THE COUGAR AND THE COWBOY

GLORIA DOTY

D1607483

Cover Design by Gwen Gades
Edited by Nina Newton
Proofread by Marilyn Reinking
Formatted by Adam Bodendieck

Used with permission:

The name, *The Branding Iron*, is used with permission of the owners of *The Branding Iron* in Mena, Arkansas

The photos and names of the members of The Hubie Ashcraft Band
https://www.hubieashcraft.com

The photos of Bozeman, Montana, taken by Mary Sullivan

ISBN-13: 978-1720892755

ISBN-10: 172089275X

ACKNOWLEDGMENTS

I want to acknowledge individuals who shared their insights and expertise.

Mary Sullivan is a long time resident of Bozeman, Montana and an excellent photographer. She willingly gave me information on the area, the town, and various points of interest. Mary also allowed me to use her photos.

Shirley Burgess is a friend and the mother of Missy Burgess, a member of the band. She read each chapter as I finished it and gave me suggestions and critiques.

Hubie Ashcraft not only gave me permission to use the band's photos but pre-read the chapters that included the band.

Nicole Marie Grice-Rorick suggested the title several years ago. That suggestion turned into forty-two chapters.

These amazing individuals make it all come together and I appreciate their efforts.

Gwen Gades, cover design
Nina Newton, editor
Marilyn Reinking, proofreader
Adam Bodendieck, formatter

DEDICATION

As always, I'm thankful to my Lord and Savior for leading me on this writing journey.

I'm dedicating this novel to all the friends, relatives and strangers who purchase and read the books I write. I'm eternally grateful for you, your reviews, comments and encouragement.

List of Main Characters

Jace...............owner of *The Branding Iron* in Bozeman, MT
Camille..........owner of *Mavis' Mag*, a women's magazine in
               St Louis, MO
Will.............Camille's housemate
Danielle.........Bozeman resident, formerly of Magnolia, TX
Collier...........local Bozeman resident
Maggie..........bartender at *The Branding Iron*

List of Secondary Characters

Allie......................Camille's assistant editor
Lorna.....................friend of Will's
Mitch.........................bartender
Ken.......................one of the 'regulars' at *The Branding Iron*
Dean.....................Danielle's dad
Cal & Lucy Frasier......friends of Danielle's from Magnolia, TX
Luke.....................grandson of Cal & Lucy Frasier
Barbara..................Camille's mother

ADDITIONAL BOOKS BY GLORIA DOTY

Not Different Enough
The story of 30 years of life with her daughter who has a
diagnosis of autism, Asperger's and mild intellectual
disabilities.

A Bouquet of Devotions
(Co-authored with Jeanette Dall)

50 color images of 50 common flowers accompanied by 50
unique devotions

The Magnolia Series
Bring a Cowboy Home
Loving a Cowboy
Riding With a Cowboy
Following a Cowboy

Children's Picture Books
Emily Jean and Fred
Elizabeth's Blue Shoes
Joseph's Dragon
Joshua and the Baseball Game

All available from Amazon
https://tinyurl.com/ya9zl7jb

CHAPTER 1

"HAVE A BEER, Jace. Maybe that'll wipe that somber look off your face," Maggie said as she placed a cold draft on the bar in front of him.

Jace barely heard her as he thumbed through the stack of bills, adding figures on a nearby calculator.

Maggie put her elbows on the bar top directly in front of him, while leaning her upper body toward him. She definitely had his attention now but not in the way she wanted it. He was trying to figure out what exactly was keeping her breasts from falling out of her shirt and landing on the papers he had spread out on the bar.

'Jace, you must be seriously lacking in your knowledge of women's undergarments. Obviously, it's been a while since you've seen or come in contact with any,' he told himself.

Maggie was a voluptuous redhead and the best bartender in Bozeman. If he was honest, she was probably the best bartender in the entire state of Montana, but he wasn't interested in her romantically. That fact didn't stop her from reminding him every chance she got that she was definitely interested in him. Her attempts to get him into bed never ceased and had become the daily talk of the local patrons. Jace wasn't too sure some of them hadn't placed bets on when the momentous occasion might occur if and when he gave in and succumbed to her invitations.

All of their speculations were going to have to cease when he told her he had to let her go. He wouldn't be able to pay her wages much longer if some miracle didn't happen soon and he wasn't a big believer in miracles. Not anymore.

He slid off the bar stool and stretched his long legs. He pushed the scattered bills and envelopes together, picked up the entire pile and told her, "I'm going to take this paperwork back to the office and then I'm heading for home." As an afterthought, he tossed a request over his shoulder, "You and Mitch lock up, okay?"

"Sure thing, Boss Man," Maggie told him. She watched him walk toward the back of the place, threading his way between the empty tables, and thought about the ever-present limp he had now. She knew it was a constant reminder of his injuries and affected every day of his life. It made her sad for him but she was certain it didn't affect his manliness, if he would just let loose a little bit. 'Nice backside, Boss,' she thought as he walked away.

Jace flopped down in the office chair and reached for a second stack of bills and notices he'd been avoiding for weeks. He added them to the ones that arrived in today's mail. Instead of sorting and deciding which ones were urgent and which ones could wait a few more weeks or months, he propped his boots on the desk and leaned back in the chair. Closing his eyes, he allowed his mind to wander back to the 'glory days' when money wasn't a problem and there were no stacks of bills to think about. His face took on a peaceful look and he smiled, picturing in his mind the long trip he made to Texas to buy the two geldings he still owned. They were superior animals and he never regretted the trip or the purchase. He also remembered he paid cash for them. He sighed and thought how much things had changed. Now, he was concerned about feeding them and couldn't even imagine a trip that long or paying that much for something.

The pain in his leg and hip reminded him this wasn't the best position for his legs. He pushed the chair back, stood up and turned off the light. Tomorrow was another day and the bills could wait. It was time to go home and crawl into his bed, even if sleep would elude him, as it did almost every other night.

CHAPTER 2

CAMILLE HURRIED TO the kitchen to fill her travel mug before she left for her downtown office. She had scheduled an important staff meeting today and wanted to arrive early.

As she rounded the corner, she nearly collided with her housemate, Will. She stopped dead in her tracks and looked at him, letting her eyes travel from the top of his head to the tips of his polished shoes.

"Well, what's the occasion?" she asked, not hiding her surprise. "I wasn't expecting you to be up yet, let alone showered and dressed."

He smiled a disarmingly crooked smile and kissed her cheek. "Do you think you're the only one with important things to do today?"

She laughed at the question. Most days lately, Will had absolutely nothing to do. Since he decided he no longer wanted to work as a stock broker or whatever his title was at a brokerage firm, he'd been slouching around the house in a t-shirt and boxers every day.

"Well, I'll give you this, Will. This look is much more attractive than the bedroom look you've been sporting every day for the last few months."

"Awww, don't kid me, Camille. You like my bedroom look. I just wish you'd let me show you that look...*in my bedroom*."

"Keep dreaming," she retorted. Filling her mug and realizing she really didn't have the time to offer, she asked anyway, "Can I give you a ride somewhere?"

Will shook his head. "Nope. Someone is picking me up."

* * *

Camille maneuvered her way through traffic to downtown St. Louis. She wished she hadn't stopped to talk to Will. Now she was going to be late and that wasn't her style. She hated it when employees were tardy for a meeting and she accepted no excuses from them. Somehow, she didn't think talking too long with Will would be an acceptable excuse.

As she waited for a snarled traffic jam to break up, she had to admit Will was still a very handsome man and at fifty, he was in great physical shape. Having an employees' gym inside the office building where he'd been employed was definitely a perk. She wondered how long he would stay in shape now that he didn't have access to all those machines and obviously couldn't afford a membership at a private venue or even the YMCA, for that matter. At least that's what he told her when he said he couldn't pay his half of the expenses on the townhouse they shared.

Camille wheeled her BMW into the spot reserved for her in the parking garage. Grabbing purse and briefcase, she practically ran to the doors. "Come on," she hissed through clenched teeth at the elevator doors, while she tapped her foot...a habit she thought she had conquered, but when she was extremely impatient or nervous, it reappeared like a bad dream.

She stopped in her office, shed her jacket, traded flat shoes for a favorite pair of heels, grabbed a few reports off the desk and hurried to the conference room.

As she entered, all heads swiveled in her direction with a few people smirking while others were outright laughing.

She took a deep breath and returned the smiles. "Okay, let's get it over with. Each of you gets 10 seconds to chastise me for being late. Considering I'm usually giving lectures on punctuality, I think that's the fair thing to do. Who wants to start?"

Then she added, "Let me remind you whose signature is on your paychecks."

After the banter subsided and everyone had weighed in on her excuse of a traffic jam, the meeting took on a serious tone.

"Jack, give us the distribution figures for last month's issue of *Mavis' Mag*. I'm already pretty sure I won't like what I hear but let's have it."

Just as she suspected, the magazine's readership was down again and subscription numbers were even worse. She closed her eyes as she listened to every report and thought she could see her great-grandmother, Mavis, rolling over in her grave. The women's magazine was named after its founder, Mavis Morley, Camille's great-grandmother. When the reins passed to Camille's grandmother, it was a thriving publication. The next generation was Camille's mother, who wanted no part of ownership of what she described as a sinking ship. Camille, being next in line, jumped at the chance to be at the helm. She was absolutely certain she could keep it afloat and even increase the subscriptions. That decision was aided by the fact she had no income at the time but an overabundance of youthful bravado.

She accomplished that goal for quite a few years, and even withstood a hostile takeover, but now she was fighting digital magazines and she knew she was slowly losing the battle.

Camille stood and paced around the oblong table. "Okay, obviously we need something of shock value...something that hasn't been done before. It needs to be a subject or study or experience that will catch the attention of our readers as they stand in line at the grocery store."

There were several suggestions that were discussed and immediately dismissed. Dory mentioned the political scene but before she could continue, Camille put her hand up and stopped her. "No...a thousand times...no. Politics is like beating a dead horse. Any news or relevancy is gone in twenty-four hours and besides, I believe our demographic of readers is tired of anything political." Dory was not happy about her idea being dismissed so quickly. She tried to hide the look of disdain that crossed her face but Camille caught it anyway. She continued speaking as though she hadn't noticed. "If I interpret the landscape and social media correctly, most of our middle-aged readers are starved for a little peace and kindness and yes, even romance. That doesn't mean they aren't politically active and involved. It just means when they have a chance to kick off their *overextended life* shoes, they enjoy something a bit lighter."

"I think we're way off the mark with the romance angle. It doesn't seem feasible to me," Dory stated. The expression on her face was daring Camille to disagree with her.

Camille glanced her way but dismissed the remark. Dory was competent and good at her job but their relationship had always been a bit like oil and water.

Allie, Camille's assistant editor, jumped in, "I don't think we'll get anywhere with peace and kindness but the romance angle is interesting. Given the fact that the majority of our readers *are* middle-aged, do you think they'll be interested in romance?"

Camille answered, "Allie, middle-aged and senior women are still interested in romance and sex. They may not be in their twenties any longer but they're not dead, either."

Several remarks were made asking if she knew that from personal experience. She rolled her eyes and continued speaking. They all seriously considered her remark and tossed varying ideas of 'romance' back and forth. Some suggestions were immediately discarded as being too risqué and others were kept as possibilities to be investigated and fleshed out.

"I realize only a few of you are old enough to be considered baby boomers; however, nearly all of our readers are of that general age. That's the group of women the original Mavis, my great-grandmother, wanted to reach. She felt that nearly all the other women's publications were for the young wives and mothers. At that time, there were very few women working outside the home, so the magazine catered to the women who were now grandmothers or suddenly had retired husbands at home. Of course, things have changed drastically over the years...I mean, for heaven's sake, we now run articles on erectile dysfunction affecting husbands and lovers, raising grandchildren, travel for newly- retired women and learning totally new skills for fun, furthering their education and yes, we are *still* discussing what to do with a recently retired husband."

Everyone in the room laughed at that remark.

Camille continued, "I'm not trying to give you a history of our magazine; you already know those facts. Instead, I want you to see how the basics are still the same...our readers are middle-aged to seniors and in today's world, they are as energetic, as committed to causes, as aware of world events and as active as their younger counterparts. The only difference is in the way they work, exercise, volunteer, read, and make love. Same females, just with a wiser, more conditioned and possibly more focused look at life. So let's think of something that may affect many of them, and if not them personally, at least it will make them aware."

Allie had another idea as she proposed an angle about online dating, and Leonard added to that with his own thoughts. "What if we had a real woman join an online dating site and write installments of her experiences and the various men who contact her?"

Michael added, "And maybe details of the meetings they have...if she finds someone interesting. It could be a type of online dating journal with new installments each month, describing the humorous contacts, possible scam artists and some serious, 'one-night-stand for sex only' meetings."

"Okay, kids," Camille said as she reined them in. "I like the romance angle but I want to be clear about a few things before you get too carried away with your ideas. There can definitely be a steamy side to our segments if we choose this topic, but we aren't publishing the magazine's version of *50 Shades of Grey*, okay?"

With that admonition in mind, they each left for their own office with lots of thoughts and ideas spinning in their heads.

CHAPTER 3

CAMILLE SPENT THE rest of the day analyzing the figures she'd been given. It didn't look at all promising. She met with the public relations administrator to examine the possibility and expense of a new advertising campaign. There wasn't time for lunch as she had another meeting with her assistant editor to discuss the morning's suggestions. Before she realized it, the clock told her it was time to head home. She would take some of the paperwork with her and look at it tonight. Perhaps going digital was the answer...even though she didn't really want to do that.

The drive home was much shorter than her morning commute had been...no backed-up traffic. As Camille rummaged in her bag for her house key, the front door opened unexpectedly. It startled her, but even more startling was the sight of Will standing in front of her wearing an apron.

She hesitantly entered the foyer, then turned and asked, "What's up with the apron, Will? Are you cooking dinner tonight?" As she noticed his bare legs sticking out from under that apron, she sighed and said, "Please tell me you have some clothing on under there."

He threw his head back and laughed nearly uncontrollably. Then lifting the bottom of the apron, he said, "Yes, my dear. I have shorts on...see? Were you hoping I didn't?"

She shook her head in exasperation at this man who sometimes drove her to drink.

"No, Will. I'm very happy to see you are clothed. I may have had difficulty eating if you weren't." Seeing his sudden smile, she clarified her statement. "I meant I would have been nauseous, not thrilled."

"Okay, okay, Camille. I get the idea. Come in and sit down, take those heels off and relax." He poured a glass of her favorite wine he had cooled in a chiller on the side table. She glanced at the bottle and realized it was from the order she'd received yesterday. She noticed he was enjoying a glass, also.

"Thanks, Will. You do realize this wine is pretty expensive, right?"

He frowned and took a big gulp. "Oh for heaven's sake, Camille. Stop being such a curmudgeon. We both know you have the resources to buy this entire row of townhouses…and you don't really need my measly contribution for the month's expenses, if that's what you're being all bitchy about."

He turned and walked to the kitchen. "Dinner will be served in fifteen minutes, Your Majesty," he mumbled as he grabbed the dishtowel he'd tucked in the waistband of his apron and flung it over his shoulder.

She leaned her head back against the loveseat. Her feet hurt from wearing the stilettos all day. She hadn't taken the time to change to her flats for the drive home. Will was an excellent cook when he wanted to be, and right now, the smells wafting in from the kitchen made her empty stomach feel even hungrier. She might as well enjoy the glass of wine and dinner, too.

True to form, the meal was delicious. "Y'know, Will, perhaps you missed your calling. As I've said before, I think you should apply to some culinary art colleges and become a chef," Camille told him as she used the linen napkin to wipe any remaining crumbs from her mouth.

"That's not on my radar, Camille. We've discussed this before and you already know my feelings on the subject. I might consider opening a restaurant, but I'm not interested in schooling or being a chef. To prepare a meal once in a while is fun, but every day? Ugh. I couldn't bear it."

Camille sighed and poured the last drops of wine into her glass. "Well, Mr. Will, what *is* on your radar? There had better be some blips on it pretty soon or you won't have a place to live."

He peered at her through half-closed eyes. "You threatening me, Camille? Are you sure you want to kick me out?"

When he used that condescending tone, she wanted to leap across the table and scratch his eyes out. Instead, she told him, "Do you think you scare me, Will? Just remember, neither one of us would look particularly good in 'prison orange' jumpsuits, in case you have any thoughts of breaking our vow of silence." She laughed derisively at the thought.

Pushing her chair back, she returned to the living room. "I hope you had your fun for the evening. Sorry it didn't work, Will. I was going to offer to help clean up but you can do it by yourself. After all, you made the mess. Oh, by the way, dinner was delicious...my compliments to the chef." She emphasized the word chef, for his benefit as she knew it would piss him off.

Camille spread the papers she brought home across the coffee table trying not to be distracted by the clanging and banging noises coming from the kitchen. Finally all was quiet and an apologetic Will plopped down beside her on the couch.

"I'm sorry, Love. You drive me to frustration. Why are you so cold-hearted toward me? What have I done? I know I haven't been keeping up my end of the finances, but I try to make up for it in other ways. I cooked dinner for you tonight and you were unappreciative, I must say."

Camille leaned back and looked at him. "You just don't get it, do you?"

Will sighed. "Apparently not. What am I supposed to be getting?"

"You know, we were very good friends for many years. We should have remained friends and not tried to be anything else...like co-habitants of a house. We argue like husband and wife but don't enjoy any of the perks of marriage. Now that you quit your job or got fired or whatever, it is really putting a strain on what little friendship we have left."

He turned her body sideways with her back to him so he could rub her shoulders and then whispered in her ear, "We could enjoy some of those perks if you'd just let your sanctimonious morals go for a little while. We could be friends *and* lovers, Camille, with no strings attached." His lips were warm as he brushed them along her neck. "Let yourself go for once. I guarantee I would more than pay my way," he murmured.

Maybe it was the wine or her exhaustion but the room seemed abnormally warm. She closed her eyes and leaned back against him. She was keenly aware of all her senses: the feel of the plush carpet under her bare feet, the dim lighting, the soft strains of a favorite classical song, the fragrance of the fresh floral arrangement on the mantle. She could smell him, too. It was a strong manly, earthy scent. They all combined to remind her of someone she had loved long ago. Will's hands felt warm on her back and her arms as he encircled her and his hands slowly made their way to her breasts. She ached to be with him for the night but instead pulled away and stood up.

"It won't work, Will...not yesterday, not tonight, not ever. Remember our agreement."

He watched her walk up the stairs and wished he could convince her to be his. "Damn the agreement! Someday, Camille," he said under his breath, "it will work, if only for one night and even if it takes a bit of blackmail."

CHAPTER 4

JACE GROANED AS he realized how late it was. The sun was already up and shining in his bedroom windows, nearly blinding him. He tossed and turned all night but must have finally fallen asleep a few hours ago. That certainly made for a short night. At age 42, his body often felt like he was 72...maybe even 102, he thought ruefully.

Throwing the covers back, he stretched and then gingerly swung his bad leg out of bed first. The stiffness was always the worst in the morning. After a few hours and a bit of exercise, the muscles loosened up and the pain diminished.

First things first...he made his way to the kitchen and the coffee pot. Taking a shower while it brewed, he made a decision. Today, he was not going to think about the bills or the bar or his monetary predicament. He was going to play hooky and go for a very long, leisurely ride.

Before he could leave, he had to make a phone call he'd been dreading and putting off for months. The call was answered on the second ring.

"Hello? This is Calvin Frasier."

Jace swallowed hard. "Yes, Mr. Frasier, this is Jace Matthews...from Bozeman, Montana. Do you remember me?"

"Well, Jace, of course I remember you. You purchased two of the finest horses we had. Are you looking to buy a few more?"

Jace laughed nervously. "No. Not exactly. You know I was more than pleased with the two I bought from you, but some unexpected events have sort of taken over my life and I'd like to ask a huge favor, if I may."

They talked for an hour, discussing the events Jace referred to and Cal's children and grandchildren. Finally, they agreed to talk again in a few weeks after Cal discussed Jace's proposal with his son, Ben, who was taking over a large share of the ranch responsibilities these days.

Jace breathed a bit easier now that he'd made the phone call. Even though Cal said Ben was taking over the ranch, Jace was certain Cal still had the final say in most decisions. He walked to the barn feeling as though a great weight had been lifted off his shoulders.

He saddled one of his geldings and placed the supplies on the other. He would ride one on the way to his destination and use the other as his pack horse. Then he would switch them on the way back. They needed some exercise and so did he. When he was riding, he could let his mind wander and pretend he was still taking groups of people on trail rides or guiding groups of hunters and fishermen to their favorite spots.

When he had the horses ready to go and their grain packed, he grabbed some provisions for himself and his dog and stuffed them in his saddle bags. Filling his thermos with hot coffee, he mounted Jesse, his favorite of the two, and leading Jasper, he headed towards the government land, operated by the Bureau of Land Management, also known as BLM land that bordered his 80-acres. His property was too small to be called a ranch in Montana but too big to be just a parcel and he absolutely detested the word, *ranchette*, as some people liked to call the smaller spreads. To him, that sounded like something 'Barbie and Ken' would own. He lovingly referred to his small acreage as his homestead. There were many memories here and it would break his heart if he had to sell it to survive.

Jace's injuries allowed him to ride for only a few hours before he had to rest or walk a bit. That was the reason he had to give up the very lucrative business of trail rides and guide trips. No one wanted to stop that frequently; it would take all day to reach camp.

Even though no structures could be built on the government land, he had permission to take groups on day trips. They rode and enjoyed the wilderness experience during the day and returned to the cabin, which was on his personal land, in the evening. Sadly, the majority of the people he took out, with the exception of the hunters and fishermen, were unfamiliar with the term "roughing it," and wouldn't have the first idea of how to pitch a tent or build a campfire.

He dismounted and sat on a flat boulder. Pouring some of the coffee into his cup, he closed his eyes for a few minutes. Remembering the different groups he'd been hired to take on week-long wilderness adventures, one group in particular always came to mind, even when he willed it to disappear.

It was a group of eight adults, five men and three women. They all worked for the same brokerage firm in California. He had some good buddies in Silicon Valley and they kept him busy with groups they referred to him. The individuals in those groups were the "new rich" and they all had more money than they knew what to do with. This particular group had been given a 'Week in the Wilderness' as a reward for their exceptional work on the account of a high-profile client. They were the usual know-it-alls, even though they were definitely greenhorns. One of the women was particularly outspoken but sweet and attentive to him. To top it off, she was drop-dead gorgeous. Her name was Lorna and she had it all, it seemed. It wasn't long before she had a piece of his heart, too.

Jace shook his head to clear the memories. It didn't do anyone any good to relive the past. It was over...long ago and far away. He might as well ride for a bit longer until he reached the cabin. The scenery was breathtaking and he never tired of soaking it in. He loved Montana, especially Bozeman and the surrounding countryside. This was truly God's country. He frowned at that description. Once upon a time, he had been a firm believer in God and he would have described his faith as strong. Who could possibly live here and not believe there was a God?

He had to admit he still realized there was a Creator of all this, but that was as far as his faith went these days. The God he used to believe in heard prayers and answered them; he didn't turn a deaf ear to his children's pleas.

When he reached the cabin, he put his horses in the stable. It was quite large since it had been constructed to hold all the horses for the groups he took out. Sometime during the ride today, he changed his mind about this being a one-day trip and made the decision to stay overnight at the cabin. After relieving the horses of saddles and supplies, he brushed them and as always, he talked to them as he worked.

"Well, Jasper, does this bring back memories for you like it does for me? Yeah? I know, those were good times, huh? You and Jesse and me...we worked good together. You know, I wouldn't have had to bring you both today... but I wanted to have this last outing with just the three of us." Jace continued talking in a soft voice. "This is going to kill me, Jasper, but we're going to have to part ways, Buddy. Soon, I'm afraid. I can barely afford to feed one horse and I will keep Jesse with me. But if it's any consolation, you'll be going back to your first home in Texas. I spoke to the ranch owner and he said he would take you back and give you a good home for the rest of your life. Now, I have to figure out a way to get you there." Jace laid his head on Jasper's neck and unashamedly shed a few tears.

Turning to look at both horses, he told them, "We'll wander around out here for a couple of days, okay, boys? I told Maggie and Mitch where I was going. I'm sure they can take care of things."

CHAPTER 5

CAMILLE MADE CERTAIN she was more than early for the next 'meeting of the minds.' She didn't want to be admonished for her tardiness again, even if it was in jest.

When the staff was gathered in the conference room, she asked each one for their ideas about the romance concept and the online dating idea or any other new proposals. She didn't give her two cents worth yet as she liked to hear everyone else's take on things first. That way they would be truthful and not swayed by her opinions.

It seemed to take an inordinate amount of time to reach a decision about combining the two ideas. Some, like Dory, insisted it couldn't be done successfully and still interest the readers.

"I appreciate all the ideas and I believe we can combine many of them into a viable project. It will take some doing and many loose ends will need to be tied up, but yes, I think the *online dating diary* option is the way we'll go. Now I need to know, truthfully, how many of you have any experience with online dating?"

They all looked at each other, expecting someone to say something. No one said anything. They only shook their heads.

"Oh, come on," Camille admonished. "This is no time to be bashful. It's not like I'm asking for a show of hands of which one of you robbed a bank last week."

Drake finally spoke. "My girlfriend signed me up once as a joke but I didn't renew the membership. And I never contacted any of the women who contacted me. But we had some laughs while reading their profiles."

"Wow." Camille said. "That's about all I can think of to say. Just wow. I thought with this many people, it would be a slam dunk to find the right sites and work out the details. Maybe this isn't a good idea, after all."

Allie shook her head, saying, "No, no, don't stop before we even get started. You don't have to be a professional dating site subscriber to figure this out, Camille. It's people looking to hook up with other people…not rocket science."

Most of them agreed with her and were anxious to get the ball rolling. They discussed a title for the series of installments and made the decision to publish one each month for six months. The readers would be promised 'real-life' scenarios from a woman who would be actively subscribed to a dating site and who would write about the men who contacted her and also any meetings or dates that might be the results of those meetings.

Allie added, "You know, there are all kinds of dating sites and some of them even cater to 'senior' people. I think our mystery dater should be the same age as our readers. That way there will be some credibility to her encounters. Our readers don't want to read about 20-year-olds dating; I think they will love it if it's someone they can relate to."

They all heartily agreed with her. They were researching the best sites on their phones when Drake stopped and said, with some concern in his voice, "We're all forgetting one thing. Where are we going to find a middle-aged woman who will go along with this scheme? She has to be single, obviously…attractive, savvy enough to keep herself safe, have a background in journalism…I mean, we don't want to spend all our time re-writing the things she sends us... and can afford to spend six months on a project that will most likely, have no future after that time?"

Camille had been pacing around the room during the discussion. She had stopped pacing and was looking out the window. Her back was to the group when Drake posed the question. It suddenly became so quiet you could hear the proverbial pin drop. She turned to see what was going on to find every person in the room looking directly at her.

"What?" she asked, frowning. "I think that was a legitimate question and while it may take a bit of searching, I don't think it's impossible to find that person."

Each of them had a rather conspiratorial smile tugging at their lips when she finally realized what they were proposing. "Oh no. Oh, hell, no!" was her retort. "That is not going to happen. There are too many people in and around St Louis who know me. Where would I ever go out with someone and not run into an acquaintance? And if my little bit of research is correct, you have to put a place of residence on a site, right? I thought we agreed this would take place many miles from Missouri. And I have a magazine to run and...and I would have to find a house-sitter."

"Wait...just wait a minute. We can surely overcome her objections somehow, can't we?" Allie asked the group. "Let's tear this apart and work on one aspect at a time."

Camille sat down and let them discuss all possibilities, knowing they would never be able to convince her to do this. She couldn't leave town for six months...or could she? It might be a nice adventure. She could see herself with her laptop, writing while enjoying the beaches in California or Florida or anywhere sunny and warm. Still, could she stay out of the loop and not contact anyone for that long? Who could she trust enough to run things?

She was pulled out of her reverie by Allie's voice. "Doesn't your mother own a house in Montana, Camille?"

She nodded. "Yes, she does but she's never there. She spends nearly all her time in Paris."

"Perfect!" was the reply from several staffers.

"Wait! Just wait a minute. I don't even speak to my mother and you want me to nonchalantly say, 'Oh, gee, Mom, can I live in your house for half a year?'"

They ignored her objection and continued as though she hadn't spoken.

"Now we need to find you a new identity. It shouldn't be too difficult; fake drivers' licenses are easily obtained. You can use one of your pictures from several years ago when you had blond hair and we can make up a great profile for you. You've been saying you need some time away since Will is home *all* day, *every* day and getting on your last nerve. And since he is home, he can house-sit for you. See? Problem solved."

"Don't you think the person I meet...if I do meet someone...is going to notice I'm not exactly forty-five as I was when I was a blond? I mean, come on...that was ummm...several years ago." She grinned, unwilling to tell them she was now 56. She never thought of herself as being 56 years old, so why admit it?

CHAPTER 6

"WHERE'S THE OWNER of this thriving establishment?" Ken, one of the regulars, yelled to Mitch, who was working behind the bar. He said it with a good-humored grin on his scruffy face, as he teased Jace unmercifully on most days.

"He took a few days off to ride up in the mountains. Said he needed some time alone with his horses and solitude," Mitch replied.

Ken laughed as he filled his cup from the ever-present morning coffee pot on the bar. "I call BS. He just didn't want to see another day with all the empty chairs and tables in here. I told him how to fix that problem but he wouldn't take my advice."

Maggie emerged from the back room. "Yeah, well, somehow I don't think installing poles for pole dancers is the atmosphere Jace was going for, Ken."

"Maybe not but he needs to do something to catch the attention of all the potential customers living in "New Bozeman." They're the ones with the big bucks and they don't mind parting with all that jingle in their pockets if you offer 'em the right entertainment."

To the long-time residents of Bozeman, the influx of wealthy residents had created an entire community of shopping malls, condominiums and larger ski slopes. Many of them drove big luxury vehicles as opposed to the pickup trucks driven by most of the inhabitants of the original town. There was a huge discrepancy of lifestyle between the two sides of the town. Hence, they were referred to as 'Old Bozeman' and 'New Bozeman.' In fact, the native Montanans referred to the newbies as BozAngeles. There was no mistaking the disdain in the voices of the locals when they spoke of the residents of New Bozeman, even though the money they brought in certainly helped the local economy. It was a two-edged sword and always a topic for discussion and argument.

Before Ken returned to his table to join the 'regulars' who gathered there every morning, he took Maggie's hand in his and told her, "You know, my dear, I would be more than happy to take you away from this and treat you like a queen."

Maggie shook her head and pushed him away. "Ken, you old coot. You know that's never gonna happen so why don't you give it up? You've been telling me that for all the years I've worked here and we all know it just gives you and the 'gang' something to imagine."

One of the other men at the table, volunteered, "Ya know, Ken, I bet if you was as young and as handsome as Jace, she'd jump right over that bar to be in your arms."

The raucous laughter filled the entire room. It was a good thing there were no real customers there yet. Maggie knew they had placed bets on the date she would finally get Jace in bed and she didn't care. It was all talk and banter and gave them something to do but one thing she did know...Jace needed a woman in his life. Even though she wished it would be her, she didn't foresee that happening. The last time she saw Jace happy was when he thought he was in love with that crazy woman from California...Lorna. She fawned all over him until she realized the bar wasn't the gold mine she initially thought it was. Then she dumped him and literally broke his heart. No one could figure out what he saw in her besides the fact she was beautiful. There was no kindness or sweetness or even morals, as far as Maggie could tell. Lorna was rude and condescending to everyone unless Jace was with her. Then she dripped sweetness like honey. It didn't matter...she was gone and that was good, but he needed someone.

Turning to Mitch and talking in low tones so the others couldn't hear, she asked, "What do you think of the idea of signing Jace up on a dating site? He would certainly get to meet some women that way." As an afterthought, she added, more to herself than Mitch. "Who could resist that face?"

Mitch nearly dropped the glass he was drying. "Are you kidding me? He would never go for that, Maggie."

"Well, we're not going to tell him, Silly. Let's just give it a whirl, Mitch. What's he going to do if he gets upset? Fire us?" She looked around at the six or seven tables with paying lunch customers and stated matter-of-factly, "I don't think we're going to be employed much longer anyway."

Chapter 7

THERE WERE A million details to take care of before Camille could begin her six-month 'sojourn in the wilderness' as she referred to her upcoming vacation in Montana. She had flown over it many times but never actually set foot on terra firma in the state. Allie was flooding her with brochures and links to information so she could acquaint herself with 'all things Bozeman' and would appear to have lived there for at least a few years.

The thought of contacting her mother sent chills of foreboding coursing through her body. Asking for a favor from Barbara was more painful than any of the other tasks she was assigned by her staff. She and her mother rarely spoke or had any contact with the exception of the perfunctory Christmas greetings and gifts exchanged on birthdays.

"How exactly did you and your mother grow so far apart?" Allie asked as they were sharing dinner and a few glasses of wine one evening after work. It was a rare occasion when Camille left the office early on a Friday but she felt as though she needed to let her hair down a bit before she left St. Louis for six months. She invited Allie to join her so they could finalize a few of the details of the magazine.

One of those details was to remove Camille's picture from the inside front page where it always accompanied a short blurb she wrote about the feature articles in that month's issue. For the next six months, the page would simply have her name and her title: Owner and Editor-in-Chief. The online dating articles she submitted would merely have a by-line with her newly assigned fake name, Emily Hasbro.

Camille gazed into her glass while she slowly swirled the red liquid in a circle, trying to articulate an answer to Allie's question. "Well, Allie, my friend, it happened like this: I refused to sell the magazine and do something productive...as she called it...with my life. Barbara hates it when anyone crosses her and especially, if that someone is *a product of her body*, as she reminded me quite often." Before Allie could say a word, Camille continued, talking to herself. "That statement always made me laugh because I'm not sure if she wanted me to know she suffered great pain while birthing me or if she wanted me to know that she actually had sex with a man at some point in her life...presumably, my father, although I've never met him."

Allie wasn't sure how to respond to that information so she opted to stick with the safer stuff.

"But, I don't understand. Surely owning and running one of the best women's magazines is considered something productive."

"Not if it isn't the biggest and best women's magazine. *Mavis' Mag* is a small fish in a big pond and I like it that way. As you know, our distribution area is tiny compared to the major players in the magazine world. My mother, because of her mother and grandmother, had a lot of pull or influence at some of the major publishing houses and nationally distributed magazines. She insisted I take a position with one of them. She constantly reminded me of the status of *Mavis' Mag* and how, without her monetary help, it would flounder and fail. She said it was a dying rag and no woman wanted to read anything written for 'old people.' I'm convinced she wanted me and the magazine to fail. I was young and cocky and absolutely certain I could make it successful, so I told her to take her money and her influence and jump off a bridge with them." After a short pause, she continued, "It's been a long time, but I may have even said I hoped her money would weigh her down when she jumped and she would drown."

Allie's eyes had grown bigger with each sentence. "Well, I suppose that explains the distance between the two of you."

Camille laughed out loud. "Yep, I believe you could assume that. Now you know how reluctant I am to ask for the keys to her house."

Allie sighed. She had never known all those facts before. Camille rarely was that talkative, especially about her personal life. It must be the wine tonight. "I suppose we could rent a place for you to live. I just thought it would be so much simpler if it could be an established address and...you know"...her voice trailed off.

"Don't look so defeated, Allie. I never said I wouldn't do it. I'm just trying to figure out what cock-and-bull story I'm going to feed her. And then there's the story I'm going to give Will. That will at least have to be plausible. I mean, he may be infuriating but he isn't stupid."

They finished their dinner and after enough time elapsed for the effects of the alcohol to wear off and make it safe to drive, they each went home.

When Camille entered the front hallway, she thought she heard noises coming from the living room. Moving in that direction, she was caught off guard by the sight of Will and some woman quickly standing up from their previous positions on the couch...which she assumed were horizontal before she interrupted. She was just happy they were both fully clothed.

"Camille..." Will said, sounding surprised. "I...we...didn't expect you home so early. You usually work late on Friday evenings."

"Usually is such a misunderstood word, isn't it, Will?"

She crossed the few steps to where they were standing and extended her hand to the flustered younger woman. "Hello. I'm Camille, Will's housemate. And your name is?"

The buxom blond with her make-up now smudged, ignored the proffered hand and quickly bent over to pick up her shoes. "I'd better be going. It's getting late and you have to be at work early tomorrow, right, Will? Isn't that what you told me?"

Camille said nothing but raised an eyebrow in Will's direction, waiting for his response to that statement. When he said nothing, she decided to alleviate the awkwardness and agree. "Yes, Will is a good employee. He always likes to be punctual when it comes to his employment."

Will walked toward the front door, almost pushing the woman in front of him, while quickly calling a cab. They waited in the front hall and unfortunately spoke in such low voices, Camille couldn't overhear the conversation. It was okay. She really didn't care what they were saying anyway.

When Will came back into the room, Camille was sitting in the recliner with her shoes kicked off. She offered her take on his evening. "Dinner...one-hundred bucks, wine...fifty bucks, cab...thirty bucks...but the expression on your face when I walked in...priceless."

Will was not amused. "Camille, you are unbelievable. You can wreck any and all of my dates without even trying, it seems."

He flopped down on the couch and stretched out. "Yes, the evening was expensive and now it is money down the drain."

"In other words, you spent all that cash and didn't even get her into bed...is that what you're telling me? Maybe you should have spent a bit more and rented a nice hotel room. You can't blame me for coming home. I do live here, you know."

"No. That's not what I meant. I met Lorna several months ago and we seemed to click. She's involved with stocks and bonds and money trading in California. She was in town for a convention and a friend introduced us. I thought perhaps she could help me find a position with the firm she works for. I told her I was thinking of changing jobs. I didn't exactly tell her I was unemployed at the moment."

"So ask her out again and don't bring her here this time."

"She's going home tomorrow morning. I'll probably never see her again."

They were both silent for a while. Finally, Camille spoke.

"Do you remember Allie, my assistant editor? You met her last year at the Christmas party. She's beautiful, lots of fun, witty and single, and the best part is I think she has a crush on you."

Will perked up a bit but then asked, "And she's like twenty, right?"

Camille laughed. "No, she is not. I believe she is thirty-five. That's perfect for a good-looking fifty-year-old man like you. Why don't I set you up with her? You could forget about your 'Lorna' from California." She paused for a minute, then continued, "That sounds like a song title or something, doesn't it?"

"Go to bed, Camille. You've had too much wine tonight. I'd love to take advantage of that fact but I won't since I'm pretty sure I'd get shot or knifed or poisoned or something equally lethal."

"Yes, of course...especially since I don't own a gun or a knife. Although, there is that bottle of arsenic I keep for just such occasions."

As she climbed the stairs, she told him. "I have something I need to talk to you about in the morning, Will."

CHAPTER 8

THE TWO DAYS spent in the mountains with his horses and the wildlife were idyllic and passed too quickly, in Jace's opinion. If it was possible, he would spend the rest of his days there and never go home but that was, of course, improbable and impossible. He never saw himself as the hermit type, but in the last few years, he was becoming more and more reclusive. It wasn't a good thing and he knew it, but there didn't seem to be anyone or anything that interested him. He had enough psychology courses in college to recognize growing depression and the devastating effects it can have on a person.

As he saddled the horses, he spoke to himself and to them, "It's a good thing you two are here with me. Otherwise, I'd be talking to myself and then I would really be in trouble." He laughed at his own joke, finished packing and called the dog. "Is everything ready, Jake? I've cleaned camp, got our little bit of garbage with me, packed our few supplies for the trip home and have a thermos of coffee. Okay, fellas, let's roll...no, let's ride. We'll take it nice and slow and enjoy this last trip with you, Jasper."

Jace knew the fact that he would be surrendering his horse was definitely adding to his despair. They had been together for years and it would be akin to cutting off his arm. It helped to know that Cal Frasier was a man of his word and would never re-sell Jasper. If he were still a praying man, he would ask God to provide some way to fund the long trip to Texas. He still had some resources but didn't want to use his last bit of funds to make a non-paying trip.

He hadn't turned his phone on in the two days he was gone but as he got closer to home, he did and although he usually didn't have many e-mails, his inbox seemed to be overflowing with messages. "What the heck?' he muttered aloud. "I don't recognize any of these names."

He opened a few and read the messages. They all seemed to be from females who wanted him to contact them. His account must have been hacked. Great.

When Jace walked into *The Branding Iron* he was pelted with a chorus of greetings.

"Hey, look who's back," Ken called out. "The wandering cowboy."

Ralph, another regular, hailed him with the news they had all taken good care of the bar in his absence.

"Somehow, that isn't exactly comforting to me, Ralph." Jace shot back.

He seated himself at the bar and called Maggie over. "You're much more of a techie than I am and know more about that stuff than I do. I've obviously been hacked. Can you help me with changing my password and all that?"

"What makes you think you were hacked, Boss?" she asked while trying to keep from smiling.

"What's so funny?" Jace asked. He noticed all eyes were on him and everyone seemed to be waiting for the other shoe to drop. The problem was he didn't know what the first shoe was.

"I'll tell you why I think that. My phone is full of emails from women I don't even know. Is this your idea of a joke, Maggie?"

"Oh, Jace…it isn't a joke. It's our feeble attempt to get some life back into you. We're tired of seeing you moping around all the time. I signed you up on a dating site. You can fire me if you want, but you need a woman in your life and you simply won't choose the one woman who is available and wants you…namely me. I'm not saying you need to get serious or marry someone but for heaven's sake, you can surely go to dinner or a movie and enjoy a woman's company." She ran her hand along his arm, hoping it might reawaken some manly feelings and asked in a sultry voice, "You haven't forgotten how enjoyable a woman's company can be, have you?"

He sat there with his mouth hanging open for a few seconds, trying to absorb the dating site information while feeling a bit hot and bothered by Maggie's sensual touch.

The guys at the front table were enjoying his discomfort way too much while he knew his face was turning all shades of red.

"Okay, okay, joke time is over. Maggie, get my name off that site. I'd prefer to choose my own women, thank you."

"That's the beauty of it, Jace. You can choose who you want to contact. Read through all their profiles and answer one. They don't know your address so they aren't going to show up here at the bar."

She turned back to him. "Speaking of showing up at the bar, some young woman in jeans and boots was asking for you this morning. She said something about a ride to Colorado for your horse. I thought you needed to get your horse to Texas, not Colorado."

Jace shrugged his shoulders, indicating he knew nothing about going to Colorado.

Ken volunteered, "She was pretty darned cute, Jace. Maybe you won't need that dating site." He slapped his knee and laughed at his own words.

Turning his attention back to Maggie, Jace asked, "Did she leave a number where I can reach her?"

"No but she said she had some errands in town and would be back in a few hours."

"Did she at least give you her name?"

"If I remember correctly, I believe she introduced herself as Danielle."

CHAPTER 9

JACE DIDN'T HAVE any idea who she was or how she knew about his horse needing a ride back to Texas, but if this was the answer he *didn't* pray about but *thought* about praying about, he was more than interested and willing to hear what she had to say.

The lunch customers were nearly all gone and most of the men at the front 'regulars' table had left to cause a bit of mischief somewhere else. They were all good men who for one reason or another, had very little to do each day. Several of them were retired ranchers which in this part of the country usually meant their sons or daughters or some other member of the family was now responsible for the day-to-day workings of the ranch. They were native Montanans and couldn't even conceive of leaving the state they loved. Harry sold his barber shop to a nephew but continued to live in the upstairs apartment because he didn't want to leave either. Ken was the most vocal of the bunch. His daddy and granddaddy had lived on the outskirts of Bozeman since it was just a blip on the map. They didn't have a large parcel of land but they made a living. When Ken's wife left him many years ago, he stayed put. He never discussed what happened and he never mentioned her name. They had no children so he had the entire house and land to himself. He let a foreman run it and he didn't do too much of anything that anyone could tell except drink coffee all morning at *The Branding Iron* and harass Jace and Maggie and anyone else he took a liking to.

In the early afternoon, a young woman entered the bar. She paused for a minute to allow her eyes to adjust to the cool, dim interior. She glanced around until she spotted Maggie and recognized her as the woman she spoke with in the morning.

"Hi, again," she said with a grin. "I don't suppose, umm," she fished a piece of paper out of her shirt pocket and read the name, "Jace Matthews ...is back yet, is he?"

Jace heard his name and came from the other side of the room. He held out his hand and said, simply, "Yep, he is." Then he smiled and continued, "I'm Jace and I heard someone was looking for me earlier."

This startlingly pretty young woman took his hand and shook it firmly...not in the wimpy way most girls did. "Hi Jace. I'm Danielle and I believe we have a mutual acquaintance and perhaps a mutual problem. I hope we can also find a mutual solution."

They both chuckled at the overuse of the word, mutual. He motioned for her to sit at one of the tables, even pulling out her chair for her. She accepted the offer graciously although he believed she would have been more than capable of seating herself.

"Can I get you something to drink? We have a full bar or soda, also. There's water, iced tea and lemonade but I'm afraid the coffee pot gets unplugged after the group of men known as the regulars, leaves each day."

She waved her hand and answered, "I'm not much of an alcohol drinker and especially not in the middle of the day, but I could use a glass of cold water if it's not too much trouble."

Mitch appeared almost instantly, like a magic elf, with a frosty mug of water for each of them and a plate of fresh fruit, cut into bite-sized segments, all delivered on a tray, which he sat down on the table with a flourish.

Jace almost fell off his chair in an effort not to laugh out loud at this gesture of hospitality. "Thanks, Mitch," was all he could manage.

Danielle's eyes followed Mitch back to the bar and then she said, "Wow. Do all your customers get this treatment...even when all they order is water?"

She was grinning, quite aware of some subtle undercurrents of something. She just didn't know what it was. She brought her focus back to Jace and started the conversation. "Okay, let me begin by making sure we are on the same page as to our mutual acquaintance. I assume you know Calvin Frasier from Magnolia, Texas and his son, Ben?"

"Yes, I do. In fact, I spoke to Cal just a few days ago."

"Okay. Well, I recently lost a mare that was going to be the foundation of my herd. Cal has graciously offered me a mare from their herd which he insisted was too closely bred to their stallion and ...never mind. The whole thing comes down to this: he and his wife, Lucy, are attending a wedding in the Denver area. He wants to bring the mare that far if I can meet him there. He also said he is getting a horse from you, so he thought we could make the trip advantageous to all parties concerned."

Jace was nodding as he was processing the proposal. "So, you're offering to take my horse with you to Colorado and then bring your new mare back?"

"Yes, that's the basics but there are a few other parts to it." She traced one of the water droplets down the side of the glass mug with a finger while seeming to decide how to proceed. "I don't trust my truck to make it that far but I have a decent stock trailer. So I thought perhaps we can make this a joint effort. Your truck, my trailer, we split all costs and we can take turns driving. That way, there's no need to get a hotel and we can make the trip quickly."

Jace wasn't sure if her face was suddenly pink from the warmth in the bar or if it was from talking about getting a hotel…or not getting one. Either way, it made her smooth, tanned complexion even prettier.

He cleared his throat and nodded his head. "It sounds like a great idea to me. I was wondering how I was going to get Jasper all the way back to his original home in Texas, but it seems as though you have just solved that problem."

She shook her head slightly. "It really is Mr. Frasier who had the idea. I'm just the messenger."

"Well, I will be certain to thank him for his ideas. Do you know exactly when this wedding is taking place?"

"Yes, it will be in two weeks. If we leave early on Friday morning, I figure we should arrive in time to do the switching before the wedding and then we can be on our way back."

"Okay. It's a deal, Danielle. Here's my phone number so we can stay in touch until then," Jace mumbled as he scribbled the information on an old receipt.

"Should I have your email address too or maybe you don't want anyone to have that."

Jace cast a 'look that shot daggers' in Maggie's direction and answered her, "Oh no. It's perfectly fine. It seems that every female in the state of Montana now has my email address."

Danielle didn't know what that meant but it was time to leave. She stood, thanked him for the water and shook hands again. "I'll stay in touch."

As she walked to her pick-up, she was thinking, *'Jeepers, Cal Frasier, you could have warned me this Jace guy was as handsome as all get out.'*

Chapter 10

CAMILLE STAYED HOME and tried to sort through all the arrangements that would need to be made if she was truly going to be gone for six months. Six months…she asked herself what kind of stupidity or desperation makes someone go to an area they know nothing about and where they know absolutely no one…not one single soul…and stay in a house that is probably not comfortable?

At this point, those were moot questions. The die was cast or whatever that saying was. She was going. She had spoken to her mother and asked permission to stay at her home. At first, Barbara was hesitant but Camille assured her it would be just her, no friend or friends coming along and she would pay rent.

Barbara's curt answer was to be belligerent about the idea. "That's not necessary, Camille. Don't insult me by insinuating I would need your money."

Of course she didn't. The property was paid for and it was a shame it sat empty all the time. Initially, Barbara purchased it as an investment and thought she might like to spend some time there during the ski season, but she could never drag herself away from her social life in Paris long enough to do that. At least that's the story she told Camille.

She did question why Camille needed to stay there. She told her it was a six-month project that she needed time alone and solitude with no distractions to accomplish. Barbara didn't ask any further questions, obviously accepting her daughter's explanation, if she even heard it.

Convincing Will had been a bit more difficult. She gave him the same story she had given her mother, only he had a thousand questions.

"Why can't you stay here and pretend you're away from your work environment and alone? I'll even make meals for you and deliver them to your office upstairs if you really want to be reclusive. I'll slide the tray under your door."

She laughed at that suggestion, picturing it in her mind. She reminded him that she wouldn't be alone if he was still there.

"Thanks, Camille. Thanks a lot. Do you really believe I would bother you if this was an important project? You don't give me much credit."

Exasperated at his childishness, she nearly shouted, "Will…think about this…I'm not talking about holing up in my home office for six days or six weeks. This is a frickin' six months' time frame. As in, half a year! Are you not hearing me?"

He raised his hands in surrender. "Okay, okay, don't get so testy. Go. Leave…I don't care. What am I supposed to be doing in these six months?"

"Looking for gainful employment, hopefully," she retorted.

"Funny, very funny. You never miss an opportunity to jab me with the monetary side of everything. You know you're going to miss me, Camille. Who are you going to say nasty things to, if I'm not around?"

"I'll try to bear up under the strain of not being nasty, Will."

"Are you at least going to give me your address and the phone number of the place you're staying?"

She'd asked herself what she should do about that but decided to be completely off the radar. "No, I'm not. There won't be any need to reach me. If the townhouse catches fire, call 911 and then the insurance company." She handed him a packet of papers. "All the insurance papers and the numbers of the maintenance companies I use are in there. That's all you need."

Will seemed truly bewildered and hurt that she would give him no information.

*   *   *

It had been agreed upon at the work meeting that she would have a new email of course, and a new phone and number that only Allie would know. If there were truly an emergency, Allie could reach her plus they might need to converse about any number of things in the course of six months. This entire little adventure was so unlike her. It was definitely not her style but she convinced herself it might be a blessing in disguise. With no love interest, no spouse, no children and basically, no parents, she worked way too many hours. Even her friends were somehow work-related so when she did have dinner with them, it was always work topics that were discussed. She chastised herself that she didn't even have a hobby or any outside interests.

When she was honest and doing self-evaluation exercises, she knew her lifestyle wasn't healthy. She took the time to stay in great shape physically but not mentally or emotionally or spiritually. With that frame of mind, she packed what she thought were the essentials. She would purchase anything else she needed when she arrived. After all, her tailored work suits were probably not the haute couture of the typical Bozeman resident.

"Can I at least drive you to the airport?"

"I've already made arrangements for a cab. But thank you for the offer. By the way, I forgot to ask, how did your date with Allie work out?"

She was interested in his take on the dinner date. She already knew Allie's opinion.

"It was all good. She's an interesting conversationalist, she has a sense of humor, and she doesn't seem stuck on herself like some of the women I've dated. It doesn't hurt that she's also quite attractive but not in an over-the-top kind of way. She seemed very natural."

"Yes, that's Allie. She is the best. She was impressed with you, too, Will. I'm happy it went well."

She didn't tell him that Allie thought he was a gorgeous specimen of manhood with an infectious smile, good manners and was a truly fun date. Camille didn't want his head to get too big.

She packed and unpacked and packed again over the next few days. Would she need any heavy clothing or jackets? Would she need some western-type garb? What about dressy outfits in case one of her 'dates' wanted to go dancing or to a fancy restaurant? She made a final decision...whatever she needed beyond normal clothing, she would purchase when she got there. At the last minute, she grabbed her favorite red stilettos and squeezed them into the bag. They were her 'comfort' shoes and maybe she would have a chance to wear them.

Finally it was the day of her flight and although she was a bit apprehensive, she was ready for this journey into the unknown.

Will carried her few bags to the cab. Then he encircled her in his arms, pulled her close and kissed her...long and hard. "I don't want you to forget me, Camille. You know I love you...always have and always will. Nothing will ever change that. Maybe in six months, you will remember how you felt about me, too, once upon a time."

She thought about his words as the driver made his way through traffic to the airport. Her thoughts took an unexpected turn. *'Maybe I should revisit my relationship with Will when I return. The two of us had some good times and we know each other so well.'*

Camille ran her tongue over her lips...one thing was certain...Will's kisses still drove her to distraction. There was no denying that.

CHAPTER 11

"GOOD MORNIN' BOSS," Maggie greeted Jace when he walked out of the back office. She paused for a minute, then continued, "You look terrible. What happened? Did you sleep here all night?"

"Thanks, Maggie. Who needs a mirror when they have you around to assess their looks? No, I didn't sleep here last night. I went home."

She pursed her lips and cocked her head to one side. "A bit testy this morning, aren't we? I keep tellin' you to check out some of the women on the dating site. I think a good roll in the hay would be just what the doctor ordered for you."

Jace wasn't smiling at her remarks. "That's the problem. I did check out some of the ones who contacted me. I was up most of the night, doing just that. Do you have any idea how many females advertise themselves on those sites?"

Mitch joined the conversation. "They're not all bad, Jace. My friend in Nebraska met his wife on a dating site and they've been happily married for 6 years. You have to weed out the scammers and the crazies and then contact some of the ones that are left."

Jace shook his head in disbelief and frustration. "I can't believe there are that many individuals out there who are looking for someone. I'm not sure having a date is worth this much trouble."

"You don't expect us to feel sorry for you, do you?" asked Ken from the front table. "There's a whole slew of lonely women right here in Bozeman. You need to get out of this bar and out of your barn and go looking for them."

"Is that the voice of experience talking, Ken? How many dates have you had in the last five years?" Jace countered.

Everyone joined in and gave Ken a hard time. In the middle of their exchanges, the door to *The Branding Iron* opened and a stout man in a perfectly tailored suit walked in.

The room became eerily quiet. Even the regulars didn't have anything to say.

He headed straight to Jace and sat down at the bar next to him. After ordering a shot of whiskey and downing it immediately, he smiled and said quietly, "Hello Jace. Are you ready to sign the papers yet?"

Jace asked, "Isn't it a bit early to be downing shots, Blakely? Even for you?"

"I wanted to celebrate early. I knew today was going to be my lucky day. You would come to your senses and accept my offer for this establishment. I even had my attorney draw up the papers and I hired an architect to design the new and improved restaurant I'm going to build on this property…after I tear this one down." He smiled a toothy grin as he glanced around the room. "Yes, I would say Bozeman could use some new eateries on this side of town. Don't you agree, Jace?"

It was all Jace could do to keep from picking Blakely up by the seat of his pants and his shirt collar and tossing his carcass into the street. Instead, he told him, "I hate to disappoint you but you've made a trip for nothing. I told you the last time you were here *The Branding Iron* isn't for sale…not then, not now and not in the future. And even if it was…I wouldn't sell to you."

Blakely smiled. "Oh you're going to sell to me. Maybe not today, but at some point when the creditors get ready to take it out from under you, you'll be more than happy to take my generous offer. And all that bullshit you spew out about how this is a landmark and it would destroy this part of Bozeman and there's so much history in this place...I'll try to shed a few tears as the bulldozers demolish the joint." With that, he stood up and walked out.

It was still deathly quiet. Everyone knew the very real possibility of what he said and that it could become a reality. The bar was in financial trouble and no one knew exactly how to help Jace avoid the dire consequences Blakely was talking about.

"I'm going home for a bit, Mitch. I've got some phone calls to make," Jace stated as he left.

*　*　*

"Okay, guys, how are we going to help him?" Ken asked when they knew he was gone. "Anybody got a few hundred thousand laying around that you'd like to part with?"

They shook their heads at that suggestion but continued to think of possibilities.

"What about setting up one of those Go Fund Me pages? There's a lot of people who wouldn't want to see this building torn down and might contribute."

"Yeah, maybe that would work. How about the Bozeman Historical Society? Think they could help?"

"Probably not," was the answer.

They continued talking but made no progress.

Finally Ken said, "I'm telling you all the same thing I told Jace. He needs something to draw people in here. I know I kiddingly suggested pole dancers but y'all know I wasn't serious. In the beginning, it needs to be a group or groups who are good enough to pack this place on weekend nights. The residents of New Bozeman don't even know this place exists so there would have to be some advertising and lots of talkin' it up. I know how we all feel about the wealthy residents and we talk about them like they're the enemy...but in this situation, they just might be the savior."

"So where do you propose we find this fantastic entertainment and if they're that good, they won't be cheap. How's Jace gonna pay for them to be here, if we do find someone?"

"Hey, I came up with the idea. Now you guys can figure out the hard parts," Ken told them as he stood up to leave. "It's not going to be torn down tomorrow so we've got some time to work on a few things, ok?"

He stepped up to the bar and called Maggie and Mitch over before he left. "Why don't you two sign Jace up for another dating site? A senior one. I'll pay for it. You never know. Maybe one of those lonely older women would like a good looking younger guy like Jace to wine and dine them. If they get romantic enough, she might give him the money to bail him out. They're called cougars, if I'm not mistaken." He winked and left, quite pleased with his idea. Mitch looked at Maggie and shrugged his shoulders, "I guess it couldn't hurt, right?"

Maggie shook her head slightly. "I don't know, Mitch. He was pretty hot about us signing him up for the first one. He might explode if he starts getting notices from older women, too."

"Besides our jobs, what do we have to lose?" Mitch said under his breath. "And if it worked, he'd thank us, right?"

"I don't know. Hell, let's just do it. It'll take a while for him to figure out it's another site anyway."

*   *   *

When Jace got home, he immediately called his banker and his mortgage company. He needed to know exactly how much he still had in his savings and in the few investments he made when money was flowing like water. That seemed like eons ago. He also checked how much was required to pay off the loans he had against his property. As much as he hated to admit it, the truth was that it might come down to making a choice between saving his homestead or his business.

He would have the long trip to Colorado to think about his predicament and to weigh all the options. He was pretty sure Danielle wouldn't want to talk for hours on end and since they didn't really know each other, they wouldn't have much to talk about anyway. He could use the time to work on a strategy...whatever that might be.

CHAPTER 12

CAMILLE PRETENDED TO read a book during the plane ride, not wanting to have conversations with any fellow passengers. She had her notes about who she was going to be and the entire fabricated story of her life. She wanted to be well versed in her new persona when the plane landed.

She reminded herself there would be no pictures to accompany her submissions to the magazine…only a fake by-line: Emily Hasbro. That was the name on her new driver's license too. Hopefully, that would avoid any slip-ups. She chuckled, thinking this sounded like a clandestine spy operation or that she had just entered the Witness Protection Program. She prayed they had covered all the bases. She knew no one in Montana or any surrounding states. She had no relatives except her mother, in Paris, so there should be no danger of a long-lost cousin recognizing her. She also believed the majority of visitors came to the state for sightseeing or the excellent skiing and she had no intention of going anywhere near a crowded tourist attraction or a ski slope.

Camille, now known as Emily, still had trouble believing she had allowed herself to be convinced this was something she needed to do. Perhaps it was punishment for being the oldest person on the magazine staff. Trying to think positively, she convinced herself it would be a nice respite from the office and the daily decisions. That thought gave her pause as she distinctly recalled the last time she'd agreed to let someone else make important decisions. She had nearly lost the magazine and her freedom along with it. She laid her head back and tried to catch a nap but thoughts of that time in her life wouldn't allow any sleeping. If it hadn't been for Will, she would have lost everything...something they agreed to never speak of...however, he occasionally tried to blackmail her with the facts of their collusion.

It had been decided Emily Hasbro needed a profile picture for the dating site. She also needed a Facebook page in case any of the men who contacted her would look her up but there would be no profile picture of her face on Facebook. Instead Allie used a flower picture; a pot of geraniums, if she recalled correctly. That in itself was pretty funny, since she wouldn't know a geranium from a tulip. Her new driver's license did have a picture of someone who looked similar but not identical of course and the name on it was Emily Hasbro, not Camille Desmond. The profile picture on the dating site was the same as the one on her license. She had done some research and realized not every email or notification was going to result in a meeting, but when it did, she wanted to be prepared. Prepared enough to at least remember where she was supposed to be from, her name and her age.

Submitted articles and columns were generally accepted with a six-month lead time, however, due to the relevance of this story, the publishing timeline had been rearranged to make room for the input Camille was going to send throughout the month. Those stories would then be put in chronological order for readers to see what happened in her dating life in a 'real-time' format. At least that was the conceived plan.

Readers had been encouraged to send their personal stories and experiences with dating sites and the end results. Did they marry the person they met? Did they have a humorous encounter or possibly a dangerous encounter? Were they able to recognize a scam immediately or were they actually scammed out of their savings? And last but not least, how many of them joined a dating site for the sex aspect? Was their experience what they thought it would be or were there embarrassing encounters due to age, appearance or perhaps, technique? Camille could hardly wait to read the responses she knew would be forthcoming. As long as they were assured of their anonymity, people jumped at the chance to tell their story.

After the plane landed, Camille went in search of her leased vehicle. As she was handed the keys, the counter person said, "Thank you, Ms. Hasbro. It's been a pleasure to serve you." Thinking he was speaking to the person behind her, Camille made no comment and continued to check her phone messages.

Then she heard, "Ms. Hasbro, is everything all right?"

It finally hit her that *she* was Ms. Hasbro. Emily Hasbro. She gave a weak smile and nodded. "Yes, I'm fine. I guess my ears haven't unplugged yet."

'Great, Camille. Just great. You can't remember your new name for an hour…how the heck are you ever going to pull this off for six months?'

She spoke the address of her mother's house into her phone. She had never even seen a picture of the place. Knowing Barbara, Camille was certain it was very nice but she didn't know if her mother had upgrades or maintenance done on it either. When she finally found the address, she pulled into the drive, which was large enough for three vehicles and smiled.

She spoke her thoughts out loud. "Well Barbara, you outdid yourself on this one. Holy Cow! Did you plan on having half of Bozeman come for a party or were you trying to make a statement to your neighbors about your unending wealth?"

She checked her messages for the code to unlock the door and grabbed her rolling briefcase. She would return later to bring her few pieces of luggage inside. The interior of the house was as luxurious as the exterior...in a rugged, mountain palace kind of way. She wasn't sure if mountain décor and palace could be used in the same context but it was the first thing that came to mind. As she toured the ground floor, she made a mental note of thanks that there were no stuffed animal heads on the walls. The fireplace was enormous as was every piece of furniture. Camille shook her head in disbelief. This was not Barbara's style...Paris was. Why on earth did she purchase this humongous home with acres of lawn in the middle of nowhere? It made no sense.

Camille flopped down in one of the overstuffed chairs and put her feet on the footstool which could easily have seated four people. No sooner had she sat down when the doorbell rang. The unexpected sound startled her and she jumped to her feet.

Her first thought was, *'Who could possibly be at the door? Bozeman's Welcome Wagon?'*

When she cautiously opened the massive wooden door and peered out, she was greeted by a man in jeans and boots with no shirt on to hide his tanned and extremely muscular body.

'If this is the Welcome Wagon representative, I can see why Mother bought the house.'

"Yes?" she asked after she found her voice.

"Hi there. Didn't mean to frighten you, Camille. That is your name, correct?" He pulled a scrap of paper from his back pocket and checked it. Nodding his head at what was on the paper, he said, "Yep. Barbara said you were coming in today and I should introduce myself." He offered his hand and a gorgeous smile full of the whitest teeth she had ever seen. "My name's Collier Phillips. I take care of the place for your mother. I apologize for not wearing a shirt but I just ripped mine while planting some shrubs at the last job."

He fished a card out of another pocket and handed it to her. "If there's anything you need, Camille, just call me. I take care of the landscaping...unless you want to do it yourself." He looked at her attire and polished nails and smiled. As an afterthought, he added, "I can repair anything, I can move furniture, I can paint walls if you want a different look and I can even tell you the best establishments to purchase things or where the best eateries are located. But right now, I'll retrieve your bags and bring them in."

She nodded at him but couldn't get any words to come out.

After he brought the two small bags to the door and set them down, he told her, "I will need to come in to the utility room long enough to turn on the water. I was here yesterday and made sure your stove and all appliances were working properly but I had an emergency call from a customer and had to leave before I got to turn the water on. I thought I'd be here before you arrived today but your flight must have been a bit early."

She hesitantly opened the door wide enough for him to enter the front foyer.

"I appreciate you doing this," was all she could come up with.

"That's what Barbara pays me for. She said you're a writer and you'll be staying for six months?"

"Yes. That's the plan," she mumbled as she followed him to the utility area.

He squatted down to turn some handles and when he stood, he nearly knocked her over.

"Sorry," she said, embarrassed. "I was watching what you were doing so I would know where the water could be turned on and off."

Somehow, it didn't sound right to say, '*I was gazing appreciatively at your broad back and shoulders.*'

Collier headed back to the front door. "You probably don't have any groceries in here yet. I can pick up a few things for you if you make a list for me or if you're too tired to cook anything, I'll tell you a great place to grab a burger and a cold beer. It's in downtown Bozeman...Old Bozeman...and it's called *The Branding Iron*. Nothing fancy, but a clean establishment with great food and a friendly atmosphere. If you go, ask for Maggie. She's a friend of mine. She's also the bartender so you won't have to look far. Tell her Collier sent you."

With that, he disappeared out the front door and Camille collapsed on the couch.

'*I cannot believe the first person I meet knows my real name, my occupation and that I'm Barbara's daughter. What else does he know about me and who has he told? Judas! This is never going to work.*'

CHAPTER 13

JACE HAD MADE a point of meeting Danielle's father, Dean. He realized she wasn't a child but thought it was the right thing to do if he was going to make a long trip with her. This morning, he made a pot of coffee while he waited for Danielle to arrive with her stock trailer. He poured all of it into a thermos except for enough to fill a cup to drink before she showed up. He was extremely sad about taking Jasper back but still felt strangely excited about the trip. Maybe he needed a few days away from bills, past due mortgage payments, Blakely showing up every few days to harass him, new emails from women every day and even *The Branding Iron*. He really loved the bar and the friends he had there but some days it was too taxing to have to think about it all.

When he saw her pull into the long winding drive, he went out to meet her and tell her where she could park her truck until they returned. She backed her trailer in where he could easily hook up to it and hopped out to unhitch it.

"You back that stock trailer like a pro. I'm impressed," he told her as he helped with the hitch.

She gave him a rather disdainful look and answered, "What exactly does that mean? You expected me to *not* be able to back it where you wanted it because I'm a female or because you just thought I couldn't do it?"

'Well, Jace, you seem to have started out on the wrong foot this morning,' he silently chastised himself.

"Look Danielle, I apologize if I offended you with the first words out of my mouth. I didn't mean anything by my statement except that you did a good job. I've known lots of people...men and women...who have a hell of a time backing a trailer. That's all. We have a lot of hours to spend together and I'd rather not start the trip with you being angry at me."

She looked up at him and grinned. "I'm sorry. I get a bit testy when someone is questioning my abilities concerning horses, trailers, rifles or anything else about a ranch or equipment. I've heard it all my life and it always raises the hair on the back of my neck. I apologize...truly I do. I promise not to make this trip miserable for either of us."

They hooked her trailer up to Jace's truck and proceeded to load Jasper. Danielle could tell this was heart-breaking for him and it made her like him even more. A man not afraid to show a little emotion was always a good sign.

She grabbed her duffle bag and stashed it in the back seat of the truck with Jace's. He handed her a mug for coffee along with the thermos and they were off on their journey.

Danielle started the conversation with what she thought was an innocent question: "Have you lived in Montana your entire life, Jace?"

"Yes and no. I was born here but I've lived a few other places but never for long. I consider this my home and consider myself a true Montanan. How about you, Danielle? I haven't seen you around before the day we met a few weeks ago."

She moved around a bit on the truck seat until she was comfortable. "First things first...please call me Dani. Danielle is too long and I prefer Dani. In answer to your question about living here, my answer is I moved here about a year ago. Before that, my dad and I moved around a lot...all over the Southwest until I got a job on the Frasier ranch. That's where we stayed for years but I always had it in my heart to have my own little spread in Montana. I saved every penny until I could afford the down payment on the property I have now and..." she put her hands out, palms up... "here I am."

Jace nodded. "So what did you do on the Frasier ranch?"

Dani looked sideways at him to determine if he was really wanting to know or if he was insinuating she couldn't have done the ranch work.

"I was one of their cowhands. For a long time, I was the only female on the crews." She continued and laughed at the memory. "The thing was...they didn't know I was a girl when they hired me and if Mrs. Frasier hadn't figured it out, they might never have known."

Jace shook his head. He glanced at her from her head to her boots. Perplexed, he asked, "How could they not know?"

"I'll take that as a compliment," she answered.

"It was meant as one. My second question is why did you feel the need to do that? Lie about it, I mean."

"Well, you see, I applied at a lot of ranches and as soon as they knew I wasn't a man, they wouldn't even give me a chance to prove I could do the work. So I decided to put my hair up under my hat and tell them my name was Danny. It worked for me until Mrs. Frasier knew the truth. By that time, I was a valuable asset and Mr. Frasier didn't care. It didn't hurt that his wife is a strong woman and I'm sure she told him to keep me on the payroll." She laughed as she remembered. "It all seems so long ago now, but it wasn't really."

"Do you have a family, Dani?"

"Just my dad. My mom died when I was six. Dad took care of me my entire life. He took me with him everywhere he went. I never attended a real school because we moved around too much but no matter what time he got home, he would work on my schoolwork with me. He didn't know much about girls so he dressed me in boys' clothing most of the time. Maybe that's why it was so easy for me to pretend to be a man when I needed a job."

She continued talking, "He was a great cowboy in his day. He never drank a drop of alcohol but he smoked like a chimney. I remember helping him roll his own cigarettes many times. He was a three-pack a day man. In his defense, no one knew it was as dangerous as we know now. That's what finally caught up with him. He was diagnosed with lung cancer. They removed the tumor and treated him. It never reoccurred, but he has COPD and is on oxygen all the time. He has a great attitude and is quite active for someone who has trouble breathing."

She stopped and looked at Jace. "I apologize for talking non-stop. I am never this chatty. You must be an easy person to talk to. I won't say another word, I promise."

"Please don't think a thing of it. I'm enjoying getting to know you. You can talk all the way if you want to." He sincerely meant those words. She was like a breath of fresh air...no games and no pretenses.

"Oh no. It's your turn. Tell me something about your life. I'm pretty sure you didn't have to pretend to be a girl to get a job." They both laughed at that statement.

"No, that I didn't have to do. We do have some things in common, though. I grew up without a mom also. Mine didn't die...she left me and my dad to run off with some other guy. Sounds like a bad soap opera, doesn't it?"

"Have you ever seen her again?"

"One time, at a rodeo in New Mexico. She must have seen my name on the program and she came to talk to me. It was awkward...what do you say? Hi, Mom, it was nice of you to take off and leave me like you did."

"I'm sorry, Jace. Maybe it would've been better if she had just left it alone."

"Yeah, I guess. I don't know the answer to that. She tried to explain her reasons for what she did but it was too little, too late, y'know?"

Dani was quiet for several miles, then asked, "Have you forgiven her, Jace?"

He thought maybe he didn't hear her correctly. Then he realized he did and didn't know what to answer. Was he trapped in this truck for two days with a Bible-thumping woman? Surely if there was a God, he wouldn't do that to him.

CHAPTER 14

CAMILLE OPENED ONE eye and realized she had slept way past her usual 'wake-up' time. The sun shining in the window was almost blinding or maybe she was still asleep and dreaming or maybe she died and this was the 'light' people talked about seeing in near-death experiences. She closed her eyes and tried again. Nope, it was still shining in the window and making splashes of light across the bed and she was fairly certain she wasn't dead. Where was she? Sunlight wasn't this brilliant nor did it shine in her bedroom windows in her townhouse.

She laid her head back on the pillow and focused. Suddenly it all came back to her. She swung her legs over the side of the bed and went to the window. The scene splayed out before her was breathtaking. The sun reflecting off the mountains and the trees was a scene most people could only see in movies.

'Well, Camille, you're not in Kansas anymore. Or rather, Emily, you're not in Missouri any longer.'

After drinking in as much natural beauty as she could stand, she made her way to the kitchen. Rummaging around in the cupboards, she found an unopened and apparently recently purchased, container of coffee. She had not taken the time yesterday when she arrived to find a grocery, so this could only mean Collier had stocked her cupboards with a few essentials before she got there.

'Hmmm, handyman, landscaper, grocery shopper...I wonder how old he is and what else he's good at accomplishing,' she mused. *'I also wonder if he's on a dating site and if so, which one? Maybe he could be my first encounter to write about. That's an intriguing thought.'* She stopped that train before it left the station. *'Camille, slow down. He might be married and have six kids for all you know...although he wasn't wearing a wedding band.'*

At that precise moment, the doorbell chimed, once again causing her to jump. That caused spilled coffee down the front of her nightshirt. *'Damn! What time do people come calling in this town for heaven's sake? And who even knows there's someone at this house?'*

She'd parked her car in the garage last night hoping to gain a bit of time before anyone knew her mother's house had an inhabitant. Right now, she walked to the door and opened it just a crack. She was surprised a house this size didn't have a peephole in the front door. The smiling face on the other side was of course, Collier's. She proceeded to open the door all the way so he and the bag he was carrying could make it inside.

"Hey. Sorry to bother you again, but I thought maybe you'd want a few groceries since you didn't leave to get any last night. It's not much...some fruit and veggies and tea, in case you weren't a coffee drinker." His smile was even more dazzling than it had been yesterday, if that was even possible.

'What was it about this man that made her lose her ability to articulate any complete sentences? Good grief!'

"Thank you. I do appreciate it. Fruit and veggies sound wonderful, actually. And the can of coffee was a nice gesture. I needed it this morning."

He laughed and said, "You're going to need another cup. Looks like you're wearing half of that one." His eyes were on the wet spot that was causing her night shirt to cling to her breast in a most conspicuous manner.

She felt the color rise in her cheeks and nodded. "Yes, I am and it's your fault for ringing the doorbell before a person has time to get dressed. Would you like a cup?"

"I really should get to my first job this morning but what the heck...sure, I'll join you."

"Unless you brought milk or creamer with you, I hope you like it black."

"I wouldn't be able to drink it any other way but there is a small carton of milk in that bag," he said as he jerked his thumb toward the bag on the counter. "And a half dozen eggs. I was trying to cover all the bases," he laughed.

"Are you always this attentive to newcomers?"

"Truthfully? No. But Barbara is a good customer and asked me to make sure you were comfortable and had everything you needed."

Camille's face must have registered her shock at that statement. "Really? I find that a bit hard to believe."

"Why? I've only met her a few times when she first bought the place. Then she left for Paris and I've never seen her again, with the exception of a few weeks at Christmas a year or two ago. She faithfully sends a check every month just to make sure everything is taken care of here. Seems like a nice enough person to me."

Camille shrugged her shoulders. "Okay...it's not the Barbara I know but I'm glad she has you to take care of things." She felt as though she needed to add an explanation of some sort so she continued, "My mother and I have not had a good relationship or really any kind of relationship since I crossed her and didn't do what she wanted when I was in my early twenties."

"That's a long time to not speak to a parent, isn't it? Never mind," he quickly added. "It's none of my business. I'm happy you're here and the house has some life in it again. It makes me sad when I come in to check on things and it seems so lonesome here. It's not good for a property to set empty. I asked her once why she didn't sell it but she was evasive so I knew she had her reasons, obviously."

Collier drained his coffee cup and took it to the sink. "I have to go and I'm sure you have things to do, also, Camille."

She retrieved her purse from the chair she hung it on last night and opened her billfold. "How much do I owe you for the groceries?" she asked.

"Not a thing," he told her, waving it off. "Consider it my welcoming gift."

As he climbed into his truck, he wondered who Emily Hasbro was. Camille's driver's license, which he couldn't help but see when she opened her billfold, had the name Emily Hasbro on it and not Camille Desmond. He couldn't see the picture, but he was sure that was the name he saw.

CHAPTER 15

THE MILES SLIPPED by as the two travelers sped down the interstate, stopping only for lunch and to switch drivers. Jace was prepared to be nervous about allowing Dani to drive his truck. It was one of his possessions that was paid for. His fears were unfounded as she handled the driving effortlessly.

Since it was nearly 650 miles to Loveland, they planned on driving all day and into the early evening. The person that wasn't driving was trying to sleep. They had no mechanical trouble but did encounter a few traffic jams and a lengthy construction area which caused them to arrive later than anticipated.

The Frasier rig was in the designated parking lot when they pulled in.

As Dani climbed out of the driver's side, Lucy came to her with outstretched arms and wrapped her in a big hug. "Oh, Honey, I'm so happy to see you."

Cal hugged her, too and then proceeded to shake hands with Jace, who was slowly waking up. "It's nice to finally meet you, Jace…face to face."

"Yes Sir, it is," was his groggy response.

"Well, come on up to our hotel room and get the dust washed off." Lucy invited. "Then we're going to take y'all to a nice place for dinner."

Dani went to the room to try to make herself presentable if they were going out to eat. She hadn't expected to be going anywhere but in retrospect, she should have known better. Cal and Lucy would never allow her and Jace to turn around and immediately head back. It wasn't in their nature.

The two men looked at Jasper. "He's a good-looking piece of horseflesh, Jace and I'm happy to take him home with us. It's obvious you take excellent care of your animals. You won't have to worry about him. I give you my word he will have a home on our ranch until he dies."

Jace was nearly in tears. "I know he will and I thank you for that. I will miss him so," he said quietly.

Cal put his hand on the younger man's shoulder. "It's hard when you have to part ways with a horse that's been your best friend. I know the day is coming when my horse, Cutter, and I won't be together anymore; either due to his death or mine," he said softly. Then he turned and smiling again, said, "Let's get these two horses switched so they'll be ready to travel in the morning."

When Dani joined them, Jace observed she looked like she was just starting her day instead of like someone who had been riding in a truck for twelve hours.

"Okay, it's your turn to try to wash off the horsey smell," she told Jace.

"Don't scrub too hard," Lucy interjected. "There's nothing better than that horsey smell."

Dani stepped up into the horse trailer. She clasped her hand over her mouth when she saw the mare that was going home with her. "Oh my," was all she could say as she ran her hands over the horse's side and down her rump. She moved to her head and whispered to her, "You're beautiful. I can't even describe just how beautiful you are."

Dani stayed with her until one of the others said they were going to eat with or without her. She wouldn't have cared but her stomach was complaining.

They laughed and told stories during dinner at a local BBQ restaurant, with Lucy giving a blow-by-blow description of the time the bull had two of their grandsons cornered in a pasture. "Dani was an integral part of their rescue," she bragged.

Jace smiled at Dani. "I'm impressed. Was this before they knew you were a girl or after?" he teased.

Jace described *The Branding Iron* for them but omitted the part about the looming possibility he might have to sell it soon. He had trouble admitting that fact to himself, let alone telling it to people he hardly knew.

As they ate their dessert, Cal cleared his throat and became serious. "Lucy and I have a big favor to ask and it concerns both of you. We are planning a trip to the West Coast...Washington, specifically...and want to know if our grandson, Luke, could stay with you, Dani, for a few weeks. And Jace, even though we understand it's been a while since you were riding the rodeo circuit, we're asking you to show him some of the positives and maybe more of the negatives of making that his life's vocation."

Dani immediately nodded and was smiling from ear to ear. "I would love to have Luke stay. Dad would enjoy his company, too. Of course, the answer is yes."

Jace hesitated. "I guess I don't know exactly what you want me to tell him or show him. Do you want him to be a rodeo man or not?"

Cal and Lucy exchanged glances. "His parents are not exactly thrilled about his choice. He's still young but he's talked of nothing else since he was old enough to talk. I guess we're asking you to just be truthful with him. Describe the dangers without totally obliterating his dreams. Is that possible?"

Jace shrugged, "I'll give it my best shot. Maybe after I show him my scars, he won't need any other persuasion."

"Great. It's a deal. Thank you both. The plan is to drop him off on our way to Washington. We'll fly to Montana and drop Luke with you, Dani. Then we'll drive the rest of the way to Washington. This is a serious business trip but we're going to mix in a bit of pleasure too. A country-western band we enjoy is going to be playing at a music festival in Seattle and we plan on being in the crowd one night. On their website, they have the dates and locations they'll be playing on their way back home so we may follow them back as far as Montana when we pick Luke up again."

Jace laughed. "So you two are groupies?"

"Yep," Lucy agreed. "We are Texas groupies for an Indiana band. I bet that doesn't happen often."

Before they left, Lucy told them, "I reserved two rooms for y'all. You can't drive safely when you're exhausted. Get a good night's sleep and leave in the early morning."

They both protested but to no avail.

"This mare you can't use because of her bloodlines," Dani said pointedly to Cal, "does she have a name?"

"Her registered name is Stargazer but we've shortened it to Star."

After a moment she added, "You know I don't believe that story about the bloodlines for a minute, don't you?"

"What?!?" Cal feigned surprise. "You don't believe me?"

Dani laughed at his expression. "No, I don't but I'll pretend I do. I'm eternally grateful to you and Lucy and Ben." The tears welled up in her eyes. "I'll never be able to repay you for this kindness."

*   *   *

When Cal and Lucy were alone, she said, "You know, Honey...I was watching those two. They're both tender hearted people, they love horses and they're both very hard workers, obviously…"

She was cut off in mid-sentence. "Lucy, don't even get started. We don't know much about Jace and we're not in the matchmaking business, ok?"

She smiled at him. "Okay, Calvin, but don't be surprised if one day they decide they're interested in each other. And y'know, with taking care of Luke for two weeks, they'll be thrown together a lot."

He shook his head and put his arm around her. "Go to sleep, my Love. We have an early breakfast, then a wedding to attend and then a long trip back to Texas."

CHAPTER 16

THE FOUR OF them met for breakfast early the next morning. They discussed the possibility of taking an alternative route home to avoid the one traffic snarl they had run into the previous day.

"It really was the only traffic-related problem we had. There's some heavy and continuous construction in one area and it becomes a 'parking lot' very quickly. It wasn't good for Jasper to be in the heat with no breeze coming into the trailer when we were not moving for so long," Jace explained. "I certainly don't want to have Dani's new mare in the same situation today."

Cal and Jace pored over the route and chose what appeared to be a way around the construction. "You should be okay," Cal told him. "You'll be on two-lane highways for a while...maybe even a few hours. You'll go through some smaller towns but that's called the 'scenic route' and occasionally, it's nice to see some countryside instead of whizzing by at seventy miles an hour. You're starting this trek early enough that you should be home in the early evening, even with the slower pace."

"One more cup of coffee and then we're out of here," Dani stated.

"No more for me," Lucy told the waitress as she placed her hand over the top of her cup. "I plan on going back to the room and sleeping for a few more hours…if you're going to join me, Cal."

He shook his head and smiled, "See what I have to put up with?" he said to no one in particular.

"I wish I had someone who cared that much for me," Jace said. Then he realized how it sounded and his face turned red immediately. "I didn't mean that the way it came out of my mouth, exactly."

Lucy asked if he was married or ever had been. Cal nudged her knee under the table.

"You'll have to forgive my wife, Jace. Subtlety isn't one of her strong suits."

She raised an eyebrow. "What? It was a simple question."

Jace shook his head as he answered. "It's quite alright and the answer is no, I have not been married. In the beginning, the rodeo was my life with no time for anything or anyone. After I could no longer pursue that, I changed my lifestyle, bought *The Branding Iron* and made a lucrative living being a guide for hunters and tourists. The old injuries came back to haunt me and I had to give that up, too. There's never been time for a woman in my life, I guess."

"Well, it sounds like it's a good thing you have the bar and restaurant to keep you going but it also sounds to me like now you might have the time for a woman in your life," Lucy commented.

Jace took a deep breath and continued, "I don't know about that. The bar situation might change in the near future, but that story would keep us here until lunchtime, so I'll just leave it there."

"For what it's worth, my friend, you should do two things: pray about any and all situations and find a good woman…" Cal wrapped his arms around Lucy and kissed her quickly.

"The right one will make everything in your life seem better. I'm speaking from experience."

They parted company with Jace getting behind the wheel for the first part of the trip.

"I don't mind driving more hours, Jace," Dani said hesitantly. "I know it must be uncomfortable and even painful for you to sit in one position for so long at a time. At least if you're in the passenger seat, you can scrunch around until you're more comfortable."

He looked straight ahead. "I appreciate your concern but I can do my part of the driving just fine."

"You don't have to be so surly about it. I was only offering. If I was unable to do my part, I'm sure you would've made the same offer."

'Would you, Jace? Would you even think about someone else's discomfort? Maybe not. What has happened to you? You used to be a really nice guy.'

Trying another avenue for conversation and perhaps wanting to redeem himself after his remark, he asked, "Lucy asked if I'd ever been married and now I'll ask you the same question."

She started to laugh. "No, never been married, never been engaged...never had a serious relationship. I had a few dates when I lived in Magnolia, but it was just friendly, y'know? Lucy even helped me choose an outfit for the first one. Too many years of dressing like this..." she indicated her jeans and western shirt. "Besides, my dad taught me that if you can't do something with passion and with your whole heart, then don't do it at all. Marriage takes a lot of work and I guess I haven't found the person who makes me want to put all my effort into it."

Jace was nodding agreement. "Yeah, I figured a long time ago, I would probably be alone forever. When I was with the rodeo, there simply wasn't time. I was in a different town every weekend. You can't expect a woman to put up with that kind of loneliness. Then I devoted all my time to taking groups of hunters or tourists out into the wilderness for weeks at a time…another bad scenario for marriage. When the accident left me with this permanent limp and disfigured leg, I gave up even thinking about it."

"I hope you take this in the way it is meant…I cannot imagine you not having women fall all over you. I mean, come on…you're young…"

"I'm 42. Not exactly young, Dani," Jace interrupted.

"Well, you're not a senior citizen either. I think 42 is young and as I was saying…you're the proverbial, tall, dark and handsome man every woman wants."

He had to laugh at that. "The only woman who wants me is Maggie and she doesn't want me for a permanent type of relationship. She tells me all the time she wants to get me in bed. I genuinely love Maggie. She keeps *The Branding Iron* going but as tempting as her offers sound, I'm not into just sleeping with someone for one night, either."

"Well that's a moral decision and I'm glad to hear you have some…morals, that is. So, you've never had a serious relationship? I find that hard to believe even though you've explained it."

"There was one woman I thought I could possibly spend my life with. At least, I wanted to spend more time with her so I could figure it out for sure. Her name was Lorna and she worked me like an expert only I was too infatuated to see it. I took her group on a week-long outing in the wilderness. To say she was attentive to me would be an understatement. Someone told her I owned lots of acreage and a successful bar and restaurant. That was what attracted her interest in me…nothing else. I was extremely gullible and believed she was falling in love with me. When she found out the land she was riding on was BLM land and belonged to the government and that *The Branding Iron* was in financial straits, she went back to California faster than a speeding bullet." He looked over at Dani. "And that, my new friend, is the extent of my love life. Sad, isn't it?"

They both laughed. "I think we're smart to stick with horses. They don't break your heart...well, unless you have to part with one or they die," Jace commented.

Dani looked out her window, pretending to watch the scenery and also to hide the few tears that escaped and slid down her cheeks but Jace noticed.

"I'm sorry. I forgot about the mare you lost. Want to tell me about her? It helps sometimes."

Dani wiped the tears and took a deep breath. "She came with me from Texas. She was going to be the foundation of my herd. She was a beautiful, smart and well-trained animal and I loved her. I had her bred and was so excited to think I'd have my first foal on the ground but it wasn't to be. I went to the barn one morning and found her dead. There was no sign of a struggle like there would be if she had a twisted gut or something. I couldn't afford an autopsy but my vet believed she had a weak heart. The strain of the pregnancy ..." her voice trailed off. "Anyway, the diagnosis was that she died of a heart attack."

"I'm very sorry, Dani. That had to be a shock. So how did you manage to afford the new mare, if you don't mind my asking?"

"I called Cal for the names of some breeders I could trust to sell me a new mare and maybe take payments or something. He called back and told me he had a mare that was too closely related to the stud they planned on breeding her to and he wanted to give her to me so she'd have a good home."

Jace gave a low whistle. "Wow. I'd say that was your lucky day. She's beautiful."

Dani nodded. "I don't believe him for a minute, like I told him last night. I worked for the Frasiers long enough to know they're regarded as one of the best breeders in the southwest. They don't make breeding mistakes like that. They could have used her but wanted me to have her. Since they know I would be opposed to anything that looked like charity, Cal made up the story. I know he did...even if he'll never admit it.

CHAPTER 17

IN THE EARLY afternoon, they reached the exit they needed to avoid the construction delay. They found themselves immediately on a two lane highway. It was in good shape but would definitely decrease their speed which in turn, would increase their time.

Dani had driven for a while on the detour and Jace had just taken over again. According to their GPS, they were an hour away from getting back onto the interstate.

"This really isn't a bad highway and I kind of enjoy all the little towns and villages, don't you?" Dani asked.

"I would enjoy them more if every one of them didn't have a stop light and a 30 mph speed zone. I'm getting tired of shifting," he answered.

"I meant to ask about that. Did you buy the truck with a manual transmission because of hauling the trailer?"

"Yes and no," was his answer. "It did seem like a good idea when I needed to haul numerous horses at one time but the main reason was because it was a hard sell for the dealer and he gave me a really good price on it."

"We have to take our savings where we can find them," she agreed.

"Do you mind if we stop in the next town for a bite to eat? Breakfast was a long time ago and our snacks are non-existent."

"Sounds like a good idea," she agreed. "My stomach is touching my backbone."

The *Main Street Café* looked like a clean little eatery. Jace parked the truck and trailer, taking up two parking spots and they went inside. If they thought the town resembled Mayberry, they were sure of it when they entered the café. There were a few tables with chairs, booths along one wall and round stools at the counter. They were greeted with nods of heads and small waves as they found a booth and slid in.

The chairs around one table were occupied by several local farmers or ranchers. Jace thought they looked just like the 'regulars' at *The Branding Iron*.

"Where you folks from?" asked one of the men.

"We're headed to Bozeman, Montana. We left Loveland, Colorado this morning," Jace volunteered.

One of the men whistled. "That's a helluva drive, Sonny. We seen your rig. What're you and the missus haulin? Cattle?"

"Oh, she's not my...I mean, we aren't...never mind...we're hauling a very special mare home to Bozeman." He looked at Dani and shrugged.

She had a smile playing around her lips at his discomfort. *'Maybe I should really make him uncomfortable and act like I'm offended that he doesn't claim me as his 'missus.'*

She decided to behave herself and explain. "He's a friend who agreed to help me get this mare home. It's his truck and my trailer."

The men went back to drinking their coffee and bullshitting about various subjects. Neither Jace nor Dani thought the men around the table believed the 'only friends' part of the explanation but it didn't matter. They were going to have a sandwich and be on their way.

Jace paid the bill saying, "My treat this time since you've done more than your share of the driving today."

They climbed back into the truck for what they hoped would be the last leg of the journey. Jace turned the key but nothing happened. He tried several more times to no avail. He pushed his hat to the back of his head and muttered, "What the heck? I know I've got a half tank of gas but it doesn't seem to be getting any fuel. Damn!"

He exited the cab and lifted the hood. Everything seemed okay but he wasn't a mechanic.

He went back inside and asked the men if there was a garage or a mechanic in town.

They all nodded. "Yessir. Eddie's the best mechanic in a hundred-mile radius. His garage is just down that side street and around the next corner."

"Does he have a phone number?"

They laughed and one slapped his knee. "Well he's got one but he never answers it. Says he ain't got time to talk on a phone."

He went back out, told Dani to stay put and started walking to the garage.

He convinced Eddie to come back with him since the likelihood of having a wrecker tow the truck to Eddie seemed remote at best.

Despite their circumstances, Dani had to chuckle. It really did seem they had dropped into Mayberry. She fully expected Eddie to look like Gomer and to see Floyd on the bench outside the barber shop.

Eddie wiped his hands on a garage towel he had in his back pocket and poked around a bit under the hood. "It's your fuel pump. Those darned things can just up and quit on a person. Just that quick," he said as he snapped his fingers.

"I'm glad to hear that's what it is," Jace said. "That's an easy fix, right?"

"It's an easy fix if I had a fuel pump for your truck," was Eddie's answer.

Jace's heart sank. Things weren't getting any better, for sure. "So how long will it take to get one?"

"Well, if I can get over there to NAPA first thing in the morning, I should have you back on the road before noon."

Jace turned to look at Dani. "What do you think?"

"Well, I think we better find out if there's a place to stable my horse and then find a hotel."

"Our town ain't got no motel or hotel but there's Mandy's Boarding House a few blocks up the street. I don't know if she's got room; there's several workmen from the highway construction crews stayin' there right now."

"Great," was Dani's only reply.

They walked to Mandy's and rang the bell. A middle-aged woman with curly hair came to the door, wiping her hands on a kitchen towel.

"Yes? Can I help you folks?"

"We certainly hope so…umm…Mandy?"

"Yes, I'm Mandy. I'm sorry for being rude." She offered her hand while saying, "I should have introduced myself right away. Now what can I do for you?"

"We need lodging for the night. My truck needs a new fuel pump and Eddie can't put it on until tomorrow."

She frowned and looked distraught. "I'm so sorry. I don't have any rooms available. The men from the highway are renting all of them…which is good for my pocketbook but obviously not good news for you."

Jace and Dani looked at each other and shook their heads. "I guess we'll sleep in the truck or the stock trailer. It's just one night."

"Oh you two can't sleep in no stock trailer, for goodness' sake." She seemed to be thinking for a bit. "I have an idea. I live right next door and have an extra bedroom. You kids can have that. I put clean sheets on the bed just yesterday."

Dani opened her mouth to say they needed two rooms but Jace jumped in. "That's very kind of you. We'll take your offer. How much will that be?"

Mandy waved her hands. "I don't know. I've never rented it before. How about twenty dollars? Is that fair? And my husband will show you where you can put your horse for the night. We have a small barn with a stall. There's no animals anymore but there's still some clean straw out there."

Dani led Star to Mandy's barn and got her settled in. They brought hay, a little grain and the water bucket from the trailer.

"You know, Dani, I think I should sleep out here with the horse. That way, you'll have the room to yourself and I can keep an eye on things in the barn."

"That sounds like an excellent plan but after driving all day, I know your leg and hip have to hurt, Jace. You are not going to sleep in a barn. Come on, we'll sleep in our clothes if that makes you feel better. Besides, think what a great story this will be for the 'regulars' you talk about at *The Branding Iron*."

Mandy asked them to sign the register even though they would be in her house instead of the rental rooms. She turned the register around after they each signed in, frowned a bit and mentioned, "You must be one of those modern women that don't take the husband's name when they get married. Y'know, Earl and I have been married for 35 years and I've always been proud to have his name."

Worried she might disapprove enough to change her mind about the room, Dani said quickly, "Oh no, I did it again." Turning to Jace, she asked, "When do you think I'll get used to having a new name, Honey?"

Turning back to Mandy, she smiled and said, "We've only been married a few months and I keep forgetting I have a new last name. Silly of me, isn't it?"

Mandy's smile returned and lit up her face. "Not at all, Dear. I did that at first, too. And you are still practically newlyweds. How cute is that?" She clapped her hands together.

They sat in two rocking chairs on the front porch of the house, and listened to the sounds of the approaching night. "This is serenely peaceful," Jace commented. "I think I could live in a small town...maybe not quite this small...but small. Get married, have a family, raise them far away from the evils of the big world."

"Is this the same man who never dates and doesn't want to get married? And having children...where did that come from?"

"I don't know. Somewhere in my heart of hearts, I guess I belong to the 'white picket fence' group of dreamers."

"That's not a bad place to be. I think we all would like the thought of a peaceful home and a peaceful world. My biological clock is ticking, though. One of these days, it will be too late to dream those dreams of marriage and children."

Jace leaned his head back on the rocker and thought about what a good person Dani was. She would make some man a perfect wife and be the perfect mother of that lucky man's children.

They stayed and talked for an hour or two longer, touching on many subjects, alternately laughing and being serious. Since the repair wouldn't be done until midday, they didn't have to be up at the crack of dawn.

The bed was, of course, a double: it couldn't be a queen or king, but a double. They both stood and looked at it for a minute. Jace cleared his throat and offered again to sleep on the floor or out in the stable. She shook her head and told him that was ridiculous.

"Don't be silly, Jace. I'm not afraid to share a bed with you, for heaven's sake. I'm pretty sure you're not going to attack me in the middle of the night. Let's just make the best of a silly and unavoidable situation."

He agreed and asked which side of the bed she preferred.

"I don't care which side but tell me, do you snore?" Dani asked as they climbed into bed after removing their boots.

"I don't think so, but I sleep alone so I have no one to tell me if I do or don't. If I find some woman on the dating site, maybe she can answer that question after we spend the night together."

For some reason, that statement instantly made Dani mad, sad and unreasonably furious.

"You have your name on a dating site?" she asked.

"Well, Maggie and Mitch have my name on a site. In fact I recently found out they have it on two sites. It started as a way to find me a date. Maggie says if I won't sleep with her, I have to find someone else so I stop being such a morose grouch all the time. Then they reasoned, if they put my profile on a senior dating site, perhaps I could wine and dine an older woman who would be willing to bail me out of the financial mess I'm in."

"Good luck with that, Jace. Sounds like a wonderful and moral plan…not."

She rolled over and tried to sleep. *'What happened to those morals he was talking about when he said he wasn't into one-night stands?'*

Why did it bother her what he did? It wasn't like they were interested in each other. She was ready for this trip to end.

CHAPTER 18

CAMILLE HAD HER laptop as well as her phone up and running with the available wi-fi although she did have to resort to calling Collier to help her with it. Her tech skills were adequate for her needs most of the time. At the office, if something failed, there was a tech support person available. Here, however, relying on only her own knowledge was a different story. Perhaps she should've enrolled in a few courses before she came to Montana. She dismissed that thought as she always found that hindsight was a wonderful but unproductive thing.

At an attempt at small talk, when he came to fix her router settings, she apologized for needing him again for such a small matter. She assured him she was capable of many things but she had indeed become spoiled by the availability of help where she lived and worked. It had been since college that she needed to do 'fix-it' tasks for herself. Being careful to not divulge too much personal information, she chatted without giving specifics.

Later in the day, after everything was up and running, she called Allie to hear the latest happenings at *Mavis' Mag*. There were other features besides the one she was working on, after all, and she liked to keep her finger on the pulse of each monthly edition as it was put together. That was one of the advantages of owning a small publication; she could be involved in all aspects of it.

"Is your first monthly article nearly ready?" Allie inquired.

"I'll send it in a few days. I may have to fictionalize a portion of it, Allie. Simply because there hasn't been as much action as I'd hoped for. I'm well aware of the fact my profile and picture isn't so irresistible that every man on the site wants to contact me, but I guess I did think there would be a few more. As you'll see when you receive the first installment, I've been writing about 90 year-olds or just really creepy individuals," she laughed.

"You should probably know we had a meeting and took the liberty of adding your profile to another site, Camille. If this is going to be as interesting as we hope, you need to have proposals from every age dimension and every walk of life. The new site is basically for much younger people. Hopefully that will get you some contacts. You know, the younger men who have a need for a cougar in their lives." She giggled as she said it, then continued before Camille could make a comment. "We decreased the distance, too by adding the requirement that the respondents had to live within a one-hundred mile radius of Bozeman. That should narrow the field and keep you from having to drive all over the state to meet someone."

"Hmmm, I guess you're right about the distance but I thought the first site we chose was for younger people. That is the point of this whole plan, right? To have the dating and interaction between an older woman and a younger man? Did I miss something somewhere along the line? I hope not or I might as well pack up and come home. I can write a boring dating column from my office."

Feeling as though she needed to defend herself, Allie quickly responded, "No, no, you're correct. But in reviewing the profiles of most of the men on the first site, it seemed as though they were all in their fifties and older.

That probably explains the interest from the ninety-year-olds. Truthfully, I believe those men see themselves as 'young' and sign up for the site. We made sure the profiles on the new one truly are young."

"Great, now I'll get messages from twenty-year-olds. I may have to ask for their ID so I won't go to jail. How can this be so difficult? I know…I'll make that one of my topics…finding the right site for each person. I'll title it, A Daunting Dating Task."

Moving on to another topic, Camille asked, "Are you getting any responses to the request for real-life scenarios from our readers?"

"Oh, boy, are we! I didn't realize how many older woman/much younger man couples there were out there. The responses so far have been from relationships that worked beautifully to the ones that were absolute 'train wrecks'. And to our delight, the women have not been bashful about telling the reasons why…in fact, there were a few descriptions of sex lives that I'm pretty sure we can't print."

They both laughed out loud at that statement with Camille telling her, "Don't dispose of those even if they can't be used. I'd like to read all of them."

Before saying good-bye, Camille asked Allie, "Have you had any more dates with Will?"

"Yes, as a matter of fact, we've been out several times. We saw a movie, had dinner, went to some of his favorite night spots and he's teaching me to golf. I'm sure I'll never be any good at it, but I like his arms around me when he's showing me how to swing the golf club."

"Good…good. That sounds like a relationship that's progressing," Camille offered before she had to end the conversation.

She leaned back in the office chair and tried to analyze why that last bit of information totally seemed to piss her off.

After all, she was the one who set them up so why did she care if Allie was having a good time? Plus the fact she had no interest in Will...or did she?

The contacts on the site were interesting. She had set a few rules for herself in the beginning: she would not answer any contacts that had no profile picture, she wouldn't answer any if their marital status was left blank as that was a sure sign they weren't single, she wouldn't answer any who stated they were looking for violent sexual encounters. As she drank an iced tea on the deck, she decided to revisit those decisions, except for the last one. She would answer the 'no picture and no marital status' invitations so she could describe the things women might find if they joined a dating site. She would still avoid the violent ones as she didn't want to end up down the side of a mountain or something equivalent.

As she considered all of it, Collier pulled into the drive. As he walked toward the porch, she tried to calculate his age. She didn't believe he was fifty, like Will, but he wasn't thirty, either. His body, at least what she'd seen of it, looked like he was twenty, but the laugh lines around his eyes and the way he walked and talked told her he was probably in his early forties. She could just ask but thought better of it.

He came up the porch steps and sat in the chair next to her.

"Been working hard?" he teased as he smiled that disarming grin.

"Yes, as a matter of fact, I have," she answered. "Just because I don't do physical labor as you do, doesn't mean I'm not working."

"I know, I know. Don't get so defensive. Can I ask what you write? I mean is it novels or freelance or what?"

'Careful, Camille. Not too much information or you'll be exposed. Answer in general terms.'

"I do a lot of freelancing for magazines plus I am working on a novel so the six months here is a good place to concentrate on that."

"What kind of novel? I mean, what specific genre?"

'Whoa, I'm impressed, Collier that you know what a genre is.'

He obviously saw the surprised look on her face and teased, "What? You think I'm some hick from back in the mountains and don't know the word genre?"

"No, that's not at all what I was thinking. I was pleasantly surprised that you would inquire about it, that's all. Anyway, it's a romance novel but it has a few twists and its audience isn't the normal 'twenty-somethings' but rather middle-aged women." That wasn't a total lie.

"Well unless your novel has elements of hunting, fishing or riding, I probably won't be interested. Although, if there's the right amount of romance and the right kind, I might buy a copy."

"I'll let you know when it's published...if that's before I die."

They both laughed at that. Then he surprised her with an invitation. "Camille, I've been thinking...since we've both been working our fingers to the bone today, how about I pick you up later and we grab a burger and a beer? We can go to the place I was telling you about when you first got here. It's called *The Branding Iron*. You'll not only love the food but the customers, as well."

She hesitated for only a second. She was tired of being at the house by herself and still feeling a tiny bit of jealousy about Allie and Will. Maybe this was what she needed.

"Yes, I accept your invite but on two conditions. First, we each pay our own way and second, I have an unorthodox favor to ask."

"Shoot," he said with a quizzical look.

"I know you know my name is Camille but for anonymity while I'm here, I would like you to call me Emily. Please? I am sort of hiding from my friends, my colleagues and relatives. For me to be able to concentrate solely on this book, with no distractions, I needed to go into hiding, if you will."

"Sure," he told her. "I'll call you any name you want. My memory isn't the absolute best, so maybe I'll play it safe and just call you Darlin' or something I'm sure you'd find equally revolting. How's that?"

"It's a deal," she laughed. "Now tell me, do I get to wear my new jeans and boots tonight or is this a more formal place?"

"Believe me, it's not formal. Jeans and boots sound good. I'll pick you up around seven."

Collier thought about their conversation on his way home. Something wasn't quite right but he couldn't put his finger on it...yet. He understood the whole thing about needing to be alone to write and even changing your name for the new people you'd meet, but he also thought changing a name on a driver's license was a bit extreme.

CHAPTER 19

"SO, HOW'S THE magazine handling the driving force, also known as Camille, being gone?" Will asked Allie as they waited in line for a table at her favorite restaurant.

"We're handling everything that needs to be taken care of," she answered.

"I'm sure you are. I hope she's giving you a huge bonus, Allie. After all, what would she have done if she didn't have you to take over in her absence?"

Allie brushed it off, "Oh it's nothing. I know she appreciates everything we're all doing. When I spoke to her yesterday, she seemed to be working diligently. We all have a stake in the success of the magazine, you know."

Their table was ready. They followed the hostess and ordered. While they ate their meal, Allie asked, "Have you ever been married, Will?"

He hesitated long enough she thought he either didn't hear her or didn't want to answer. Finally, he said, "Yes, I have. We were both in college, we were young and in love." He smiled ruefully. "We were also naïve and a little bit stupid."

"If it's too painful, you don't have to tell me about it."

"It was a long time ago, Allie. There's no pain associated with it any longer. We allowed some outside forces to come between us...ambition, a pushy parent, lack of employment and a few other things."

"You know, you and Camille have a lot in common. When we spoke about our younger lives one night and I asked if she had ever been married, she told me almost the same thing."

Will nodded then checked his watch. "We need to hurry if we're going to make the opening curtain at the theater."

There was no more discussion of Camille or the magazine until they were enjoying a drink after the performance.

"I've been wanting to tell you something and ask you something Allie. I'm going to be out of town for a month or more." He took her hand as he said, "I'm really, really going to miss our dates. You're different from any woman I've ever dated and I mean that…truly. You have a wide range of interests and you're easy to talk to. I feel very comfortable when I'm with you."

She felt the color rising in her cheeks. *'Like an adolescent schoolgirl,'* she thought.

"I feel comfortable with you too. Thanks for the compliment. You said you wanted to ask me something?"

'Please, please ask me to come home with you and spend the night with you, Will.'

"Yes, I do. As I said, I will be gone for a while and I can't leave the house empty for that long without at least telling Camille…so I wondered if I could persuade you to give me her new phone number. I won't share it with anyone but I need to explain to her that I'm leaving."

Allie's eyes opened wide but no words came out of her mouth. *'You rotten SOB. All these dates and flattery and making me believe you wanted me and instead you want a freaking phone number?'*

She reined in her thoughts and politely told him, "I'm sorry, Will but I can't give you that. You'll have to try to find someone else to get it from. However, no one else knows it, so that might be difficult. If you'll excuse me, I'm going to call a cab. Enjoy the rest of your drink." She placed some cash on the table. "That's for my share of the evening. Oh, and please don't call me again."

Will stood as she was leaving, "Wait, Allie. Don't leave. I didn't mean…."

She was already gone. He sat down and asked himself, *'What the hell just happened?'*

He paid the bill and went home still asking himself exactly how he screwed up the evening. *'Did Allie believe I was going to ask her to come home with me? Hmmm, interesting. Maybe I should have. Perhaps she would have given me the number when we were in the middle of making love. Does the phrase Hell hath no fury like a woman scorned, come to mind, Will? I'll have to find Camille's new phone number some other way or at least where she's staying. It's driving me crazy to not know and besides, I need to talk to her to get the combination to the safe. If she wasn't so paranoid, she would have given me that long ago. Still no trust after all these years. How sad is that?'*

His phone beeped. Caller ID told him it was Lorna. "Hello Beautiful. How's sunny California?"

"It's definitely sunny but it would be sunnier if you were here, Will. Have you decided when you'll be able to come out? I don't know how much longer the position will be open."

"Why can't I apply online? I've hit a bit of a snag here as far as leaving right now but I can send my resume and any other paperwork you need."

"Of course, that's possible but I think you'd make a much bigger impression in person, and besides, I want you here." He could hear the poutiness in her voice.

"We would have a great time, Will. I could show you all my favorite places." She laughed. "You know what I mean, right?"

When she heard him chuckle, she added, "Oh yes and my favorite places to visit and sightsee also."

"I will continue to try to make arrangements on this end but coming there in the immediate future doesn't seem like a very real possibility at this point. There's some business I have to take care of here before I leave and I'm running into obstacles in that endeavor. If you could please send me the name of the person I need to contact, I'll forward my resume to them. Also, I'll let you know when I'm able to fly out. If the position is no longer available, I'll have to live with that."

They ended the call with Will having several thoughts going through his head. One was that he needed Camille's phone number and the combination to the safe...now. The other one was questioning himself if he actually wanted to see Lorna again. She was a bit too pushy and crude, even for his taste in women.

His next course of action was to search *Mavis' Mag's* website and FB page. Perhaps there were clues to her whereabouts but he was highly doubtful. Where would she go for six months? Even if the magazine was paying, that long a stay could be quite expensive. Maybe she was living with a friend or relative. He dismissed that idea as soon as it was a conscious thought. Camille literally didn't have any friends. At least none that were close enough to let her move in with them. She didn't have any relatives, either, except her mother and they didn't speak to each other. Another dead end...she seemed to have disappeared from the face of the earth.

He went for a walk to try and clear his brain. There was something niggling at the periphery of his memory but he couldn't recall it into his mind's eye. It was something he'd seen her reading one evening before she went to bed. A travel brochure? Maybe. If so, what was the picture on the front? Mountains, evergreen trees, rocks, waterfalls...well, that narrowed it down to about one-thousand locations. *'Think, Will, think. There was a name on the front with those pictures…what was it?'* He stood still and squeezed his eyes shut, trying to will his visual memory into bringing it to the forefront of his brain. He didn't care what the people passing him were thinking. This was important. Finally, he believed it had an M-something on the front.

'Okay, we can eliminate Missouri as we don't have that kind of mountain ranges here. Mississippi? No. Maryland? No. Massachusetts…possibly. Maine?… another possibility. Montana?… probably not. It was too rugged and unpopulated for Camille's tastes.' As he walked back home, he suddenly stopped dead still causing the person riding a bike behind him to nearly run over him.

"Hey," the woman yelled as she pedaled past. "What're you doing?"

"Sorry," Will shouted at her retreating figure. "I just remembered something important."

He grinned as he went back to the townhouse. It might be far-fetched, but it was the most hope he'd had so far. Camille's mother, Barbara, owned a home in Montana. What better place to hide for six months?

He took the steps two at a time on his way to Camille's bedroom. He wasn't positive what he was searching for exactly but there might be some correspondence of some kind or an address book or something with Barbara's Montana address on it.

He rifled through the few papers Camille left on the desk. It was too bad she was such a neat and tidy person. She must have packed her address book too. He stood in the middle of the room and turned slowly in a circle. What was the one thing she always kept…seemingly for posterity? Receipts…they had laughed about it many times…her unwillingness to ever dispose of any receipts. She hung on to them long after they were of no importance any longer. He opened the top drawer of her dresser…hallelujah, maybe.

There was the motherlode of receipts. Now to find the one from the Fedex office when she mailed her mother's obligatory Christmas gift to the house in Montana. He remembered she said she was glad Barbara decided to spend a week there. The postage wouldn't be as much as sending it to Paris.

It didn't take long to find as Camille's organizational skills had them arranged by month. Unfortunately, the paper had obviously gotten wet at some point. Will was swearing as he tried to read the obliterated address. However, the space with the recipient's phone number was still visible…barely…but he thought he could read it. He wasn't in the habit of praying but that's what he was doing now…praying there was still a land line associated with that phone number. He realized most homes no longer had a land line but Barbara was the kind of person who would keep one even if she didn't need it or didn't live there.

* * *

Camille was choosing the shirt she would wear to go with Collier this evening. She wasn't accustomed to jeans and the new ones were fairly stiff but since they fit her like her skin, they soon softened up and melded to her slim figure. Looking in the mirror to assess the overall effect, she jumped when she heard the phone on the nightstand in the spare bedroom ringing. She hadn't believed it was working, but was left from when Barbara was there. She thought about ignoring it but decided it might be Collier, if he lost her cell phone number.

"Hello?"

"Hi Camille. It's nice to hear your voice."

CHAPTER 20

CAMILLE WAS SHOCKED enough she lost her voice for a minute. When she could regain it and control her temper and not let her first words be a string of expletives that would burn Will's ears, she answered. "Hello, Will. I guess your magnetic personality has managed to charm my information out of Allie, hasn't it?"

"No, no...that's not true. Don't blame Allie for this. Not that I didn't try but she not only refused to give me your cell phone number but she told me to never contact her again."

"Good for her. I'm sure there's more to that story but please spare me the details. So if you couldn't wheedle it out of Allie, how exactly did you find me and why? Why, Will? What on God's green earth do you need from me? You don't have the decency to give me some time alone?"

"Calm down, Camille. Don't get your bloomers in a knot. Hear me out and you'll be happy I have such awesome detective skills."

She heard the doorbell and knew it was Collier, ready to pick her up for the evening. She wasn't about to let Will ruin this.

"Sorry Will, but I have to go. My date is at the door."

She smiled as she said it, knowing this wasn't a date, but she couldn't refrain from telling him that.

"Now that you have the land line number, you can call tomorrow morning. Bye."

As soon as she hung up, she unplugged the phone from the wall jack.

"Wait, Camille…damn!" The line was dead and he still didn't have the combination to the safe. He had no choice but to wait until tomorrow. He poured himself a glass of Scotch and turned on the television. What difference did one more day make?

'I know you too well, Camille. You're going to unplug that phone from the wall jack and I'll be back to square one.'

He absently swirled the liquor in the glass and suddenly had an inspiration. Cell phones had area codes from anywhere but landlines still had area codes from cities. He grabbed his phone and googled the area code he had previously dialed. Montana…what? Only one area code for the entire state? Perfect…just perfect. He decided to check the prefix of the number. Surely the towns had different prefixes. This time he was successful. The prefix was for a town called Bozeman. If she didn't answer tomorrow, he would fly there. It wasn't a tiny town, but somehow he would find her.

His mind replayed their short conversation. *'Did she say she had a date? That was fast. She didn't date anyone when she lived here.'*

* * *

Camille answered the door with a smile on her face hoping she didn't look as pissed off as she felt inside.

"Hi Collier. I'm ready. Do I look okay for where you're taking me?"

He nodded his head slightly and gave a low whistle, "You look fantastic. Wow is about the only word I can come up with at the moment…Emily."

She was impressed with him, also. She'd never seen him when he wasn't wearing work clothes. He looked good then too but tonight, he was stunning…if you could use that word to describe a man. The tight jeans, cowboy boots, hat and chambray shirt were a plus although she had to admit she liked the 'no shirt' look, too.

"You remembered my name. I'm so impressed."

"Well, I'm here to impress, ma'am. Seriously, I remembered to call you Emily right now, but that might not last all night so if you see me faltering with your name, just jump in and rescue me, okay? I've never had a date with a woman who had two names."

'Did he just call this a date? That's okay with me. It's been a long time since I've been out with someone other than friends from work. I could get used to this…maybe I'll be a real-life cougar.'

Collier couldn't help but notice the smile that slowly spread across her face. "Was it something I said or is my shirt on backwards or are my jeans unzipped?"

She shook her head. "None of those things. You look all put together to me, Cowboy. Let's go find this bar you told me about."

"This is a night of 'firsts' for me," Camille commented as they left her drive.

"How so?"

"Well, I've never worn a pair of cowboy boots, I've never had a pair of jeans this tight, I've never gone out to eat with someone I just met and I've never ridden in a pick-up truck."

Collier glanced across at her and blurted, "You're kidding, right? I mean, you haven't been living much, huh? Do you classify yourself as a workaholic or just anti-social?"

She pursed her lips and frowned. "Let me think about that. Maybe both. I do work an inordinate amount of hours, I suppose, but the anti-social part…hmmm…maybe. Yeah, maybe I am. My coworkers are all younger than me and with the exception of a few of them, we don't have the same taste in food, music or conversation. We don't share the same life experiences."

"They can't be that much younger than you or they'd all be in college."

"You know how to flatter a woman, that's for sure. I appreciate the compliment, Collier but I'm a bit older than post-college." She hesitated and then decided what difference did it make? Might as well be truthful about something. "I'm 56. Now you know and if you want to forget our evening, I'll understand."

"You're not getting rid of me that easily, Camille."

She didn't have a response so she went back to their previous conversation. "I'm sure I am missing out on a lot. It's easier after a day at work, to go home, kick my shoes off, have a glass of wine and maybe watch a little bit of television with Will, although we don't usually like the same shows either."

Collier frowned a little. "Who's Will? I don't mean to pry but I've always made it a point to not go out with married women and I don't aim to start now."

"Oh no, I'm not married. Will is my housemate. We share a townhouse and the expenses. Well, we did share expenses until he lost his job. Now I'm supporting him, I guess."

"I'm confused. You live with some guy but you don't...you know..."

"Have sex?" she asked as she helped him find the words he couldn't seem to spit out.

"Yeah...that."

"Collier, are you blushing? I'm sorry. I didn't mean to embarrass you. I occasionally forget not everyone is as straightforward as I am. Anyway, Will and I have known each other for a very, very long time. We began as friends, progressed to friends and lovers, then thirty years ago, our relationship digressed back to just friends. As of about thirty minutes ago, we are no longer even friends."

"What happened thirty minutes ago? I mean, no one knows you're here. How could he do something to irritate you that much if he can't talk to you?"

Camille took a deep breath while looking out the window at the passing scenery.

"Somehow, he found a way. He called the land line that's still connected at the house. I told him I had to leave, hung up and promptly unplugged the line. He doesn't have my cell phone number so maybe it's over."

"What did he want? What if he does find you? Camille, are you afraid of him? Will he hurt you?"

She shivered at the thought but immediately dismissed it. "He won't hurt me, Collier. He's actually a decent guy and I loved him once…long ago. I believe he still has feelings for me but more importantly, I'm holding the winning card, so to speak. I have some papers in my safe that could do him a lot of harm but we have an agreement. I will never use that information and he will never divulge the details, either. It's complicated. It deals with a hostile takeover, a brokerage firm, some traded stocks, and various other semi-illegal things. We agreed to never speak of it and the only reason I feel safe telling you is because I know you and Will are never going to meet. I'm also sure that's way more information than you wanted to know."

The subject was dropped. They arrived at *The Branding Iron*, found a place to park, and Collier came around the truck to open her door.

'Aaand, he's a gentleman, too.' Camille thought.

As they entered, it took a minute for her eyes to adjust to the dim interior. There was a country tune coming from a sound system somewhere, several tables were filled and there were a few people at the bar. Collier placed his hand on the small of her back and guided her to the one end of the bar where a woman with beautiful red hair was conversing with a customer.

"Hey Maggie," he shouted.

She immediately turned her head and smiled, while coming around the end of the bar. She wrapped her arms around him, saying, "Collier, where the heck you been? I've not seen you in here in months. I missed ya, you good-lookin' devil. Where've you been hidin' yourself?"

Collier was grinning and had his arms around Maggie in a bear hug. When they let go of each other, she noticed Camille. Collier said, "Maggie, I want you to meet a friend, Ca…Emily. And, Emily, this is Maggie, the best and most beautiful bartender in Montana."

Camille offered her hand, and Maggie grabbed it with both of hers. "Well, now I know where Collier's been spendin' his time."

They moved to a table and ordered drinks and sandwiches. As they were eating and talking, a tall, dark-haired man came striding up to their table. He walked with a pronounced limp but it didn't seem to slow him down too much. Collier stood and shook hands with him. "Good to see you, Jace. It's been a while. This," he said, indicating Camille, "is a new friend and client, Emily. She's living in the big house on Flagler Rd."

Jace shook hands with her and she noted he had the most disarming smile that just tugged at the corners of his mouth, sensous lips and deep, penetrating eyes.

"It's good to meet you, Emily. Bozeman can always use more beautiful residents."

'Good Lord, how many handsome men can I meet in this town? And they both seem to be much younger than me. Who needs a dating site with specimens like this walking around?'

Turning his attention to Collier, Jace agreed with his earlier statement. "It has been a while, Buddy. I've been doing a bit of wandering with the horses before I sent the one back to Texas by way of Colorado."

Jace sat down at their table while he and Collier discussed the trip to Colorado he recently took and some other local happenings. Finally, he stood and excused himself. "I think Mitch needs me. It was nice to meet, you…Emily, right? Don't be a stranger. You can come to *The Branding Iron* without bringing this old man with you," he said, jerking his thumb toward Collier.

"Hey, who you calling an old man? If I recall, you were blowing out 42 candles on your last birthday cake, Jace."

They both laughed, shook hands and Jace went to the back room.

"He's a great guy. We've been friends for quite a while. I forgot to tell you he's the owner of this establishment. I've heard some rumors that he's in a financial bind. I hope it's not true. I'd hate to see this place sold or worse…torn down."

Camille looked around the interior. It had wooden flooring worn smooth by years of boots walking on it, the walls were a lighter wood and the bar, itself, was magnificent. It was large and had a soft patina from years of use. As a journalist, she wondered how many conversations had been shared there and how many life decisions had been made or affected while someone leaned on that bar. It would, indeed, be a shame to tear the building down.

Instead of taking her directly home, Collier drove around the darkened streets of Bozeman. "I hope you don't mind. This is a little night sightseeing. If you stay long enough, you'll hear about Old Bozeman and New Bozeman. Don't be too swayed by some things people say. It really is just one community with of course, different elements, like any town or village. Some of the long-time residents resent the newcomers and vice-versa but they also know those same people bring in much needed funds for development and progress. We all have to live together because ultimately, we all love our town and this state."

When they reached her house, he walked her to the door.

"Would you like to come in for a minute?"

He checked his watch. "Yeah, that'd be okay. I want to check that phone and make sure there are no others anywhere else in the house."

Camille hadn't thought about that. Of course there would be others. Land lines were seldom in just one room. She made a pot of coffee while he checked the entire house.

"There were two more. I unplugged all of them. I sincerely hope this Will guy doesn't try to contact you, Camille. I'm worried about you, all alone in this big ole house."

She waved her hand to dismiss that thought. "Thank you for your concern but I assure you I will be okay. Will is harmless…really. He knows I could probably get him a prison sentence although I'd be taking the chance I'd be serving time with him, as an accomplice. I think that's the charge when you know something and don't tell."

They drained their cups and she walked him to the door.

He turned to her and seemed to be about to kiss her but changed his mind at the last minute.

"Good night, Camille. I enjoyed the evening."

CHAPTER 21

CAMILLE HAD HER first submission ready for Allie and the staff to transcribe into a printable article. They had agreed she would list her experiences, send them and they could put them in the order they thought best plus correct grammatical or punctuation errors. There could possibly be many of those since she was writing in a semblance of shorthand.

She read over them one final time, alternately smiling and frowning, depending on the interaction she had with each man. She not only wanted women to see some of the honest, sincere men but also a few of the looney ones they might meet. She wanted to impress upon them the need to be smart and safe.

She began with a bit of explanation.

For anyone who has never been to a dating site: Most sites have an area where the members can privately chat with each other...one on one if they want to.

If someone is interested in your profile they can send you a 'wink' or a 'hello.' Then it's up to you if you choose to answer or not.

Don't give anyone your email address unless you want to be contacted that way. I find email is safer than a phone number.

Don't give your house address, even if he sounds like the nicest guy in the world.

Definitely don't believe everything they put in their profile information.

If they say they are from some far part of the country, stay away from them.

When they give you a real name, check to see if they are on any social media sites. I only found one who was.

If there is no profile picture, use your discretion when deciding to answer their 'hellos.'

As she took one last look at the list of her experiences before hitting the "send" button, she quietly chuckled to herself at some of them:

Denny: age 68 had no profile picture, listed his marital status as legally separated

I talked with him in the chat room of the dating site. He explained his wife had been in an accident and was incapacitated. She was in a nursing home and had been for quite some time. He wanted me to know he took care of all her needs and always would. I commended him for that but questioned his faithfulness if he was on the dating site. He said he was just looking for a 'friend' because he was lonely. I chatted several more times with him; he finally got around to talking about meeting at a motel. It took about two weeks to go from needing a 'friend' to saying we could be 'friends *and* lovers.' He described his prowess in the bedroom and I told him goodbye as I certainly wasn't going to help him cheat on his wife, regardless of her condition.

Edgar: age 45 no profile picture, single, never been married we talked several times and made arrangements to meet for lunch at a busy fast food restaurant (safer) At the last minute he sent me a text saying he was shy and could tell I was much too outgoing for him and he just couldn't bring himself to meet me.

<u>Sam</u>: age 48 profile picture showed nice looking man. He also wanted to meet for coffee but insisted it be in a different town. He said his community was small and everyone knew each other. He didn't want anyone to know he had his name on a dating site.

<u>Roger</u>: 43 no picture professed to be in the military in Afghanistan. He called me every evening at the same time, which he said was early morning there. I checked the time difference between my time and the time in Afghanistan and he was correct so either he had his facts all lined up or he was telling the truth. We had some deep philosophical discussions. I liked him and enjoyed talking to him. One day he simply disappeared. I never heard from him again. Either I was duped or he was telling the truth and perhaps he was killed in action. I was surprised how sad it made me and how I could be that emotional about someone I had never met in person.

<u>Thomas</u>: 56 no profile picture and marital status was legally separated. This one was a professor of engineering at a college. After a few weeks of chatting, he e-mailed pictures of himself accepting an award. I checked that college website and his name was listed. His story was that his first wife died and he remarried too quickly. He was extremely unhappy with his new spouse. I had no intention of meeting a married man but we had some interesting talks.

<u>Daniel</u>: 56 profile picture average looking fellow He was not married. We talked a few times and he asked for my e-mail. I gave it to him but what he wanted to send me was a list of 46 questions. I started to answer them but by the fifth one, I decided this guy was way too paranoid for me. He had obviously been hurt at some time and was searching for a

guaranteed relationship. Every question was asking if I had ever cheated in a former relationship or if I had ever lied or if I considered lying to be a normal trait. I never talked to him again.

Frank: 53 profile picture average, Frank would email me and then I wouldn't hear from him for 3-4 days. He wanted to take it s-l-o-w because (his words) 'the broad he dated for eight years suddenly left him' Maybe she thought he was too slow

Elliott: 56 no picture He lived close to me, he was a self-made man in his words and he described his work and his days, ad nauseam. He wanted to meet but never could find the time. He was very self-absorbed. He never asked anything about my day or work or family...only his. I finally told him I wasn't interested.

Richard: 62 He wanted to use Yahoo messenger so we could see each other while we talked. He called every morning around 6:30 so many times we talked while I drank my coffee. At first, it was general subjects, even some politics and religion but then it became almost solely about sex. That coupled with the fact he told me he was sitting in his office chair with no underwear on. I could only see him from the waist up, thank God, but that was the end of those conversations. (Have you figured out by now there are some really weird people out there?)

Jackson: 48 nice-looking gentleman He was a mechanical engineer and he worked for an international company. He was sent all over the world when a country needed some repairs to their infrastructure, he and his crew would go there.

Interesting. He had a son who lived in London. He'd like to take me there some time. He lived in a town not too far away, so I suggested we meet there for coffee. He couldn't as he was going out of town. We carried on our texting friendship for a while when he said he was being sent to some foreign country with a crew. He would text me as soon as his plane landed. He did and told me a sad tale of how his camera and computer and his wallet containing his credit cards were all stolen as soon as he got there. Could I purchase a computer and send it to him? No. Well, he was desperate so could I give him my credit card numbers so he could replace his electronics and he would pay me back as soon as his company reimbursed him. I told him I was not going to give him anything. I had never been sworn at in a foreign language before that day. Needless to say, I never heard from him again which was perfect.

Antonio: 42 The photo he used was that of a very handsome man. When he contacted me, I asked why a gorgeous young man like him was contacting a woman my age. He answered that he was Italian, he liked older women and he thought I was beautiful. Okay, now even when we know it's BS, what woman doesn't want to hear that kind of statement? I ignored his 'hellos' on the site for a few days but then gave him my email address. We had some interesting email conversations which led to phone conversations. I looked him up on WhitePages.com and his address was legitimate. We would talk until the wee hours of the morning. I truly liked him and he was one sexy man. He knew exactly what to say and how to say it and he assured me he also knew exactly what to do and how to do it. Eventually I told him that I couldn't continue talking to him but it would have been interesting to see where it might lead in time.

That was enough for the first installment. She knew her staff and trusted they could polish it up. She used fictitious names but used the correct ages. Now that she was on a site for younger men, it should be even more interesting. This was about online dating but specifically, the younger man with the older woman. So far, what she was sending was about men of any age, with the exception of Antonio. He was the youngest.

CHAPTER 22

DANIELLE WATCHED LUKE and her father play checkers while she prepared breakfast. She hadn't seen her father that happy for quite a while. It was good for him to have some diversion and activity.

Cal and Lucy had arrived yesterday afternoon. They rented a car and followed the directions to her house. It was good to see them again. When they returned in a few weeks to pick up Luke, it would probably be the last time she'd see them for a long time.

They stayed for a few hours, then they were on their way to Seattle, Washington. It seemed they were looking forward to the scenic drive and were anxious to be on their way. After stowing Luke's bags in the spare bedroom and giving him a few last instructions, they left.

Dani wasn't sure how she would keep Luke occupied for the entire time but there were always chores to do and he was going to spend time with Jace, learning more about rodeos.

Ah, yes, Jace...she had relived the last part of their Colorado trip in her mind more than once. After he talked about being on a dating site and looking for an older woman to bail him out, she lost all respect for him. She asked herself many times if she was being honest when she felt appalled at what he said or if she was hurt because she was imagining the two of them dating.

She hadn't spoken much after they spent the night together at Mandy's house in some little town. She couldn't even recall the name of it at the moment. They got up in the morning, returned to the café for breakfast, took care of Star and then waited for the truck to be fixed. He asked if she wanted to wander around the side streets for a while but she declined, opting to read a book she brought with her. There was no mention of the awkwardness of the previous night and the experience had lost its humor after he talked about his dating plans. If Jace noticed her quietness, he didn't mention it. Maybe he was glad she stopped talking and he could enjoy some solitude.

It really didn't matter now. They took different paths and life went on. She was supposed to take Luke to Jace's ranch so she would have to see him and speak to him again, whether she wanted to or not. It would be difficult to avoid him even if she wanted to.

'Do you want to avoid him, Danielle or are you nursing hurt feelings? You know better than to jump to conclusions, especially about men and how they think. Admit that you were falling for Jace Matthews and imagining all sorts of scenarios. Once you face the truth, you can move on. He's a good guy and you can't avoid speaking to him forever.'

"Dani," her father almost shouted, "are you going to finish your scrambled eggs or are you gonna sit there in never-never land all morning?"

She smiled. "Sorry, Dad, I was thinking of something else and forgot to come back to the present, I guess." She cleaned up the dishes with Luke's help and after taking a deep breath, she called Jace's number.

Jace answered on the second ring when he saw the caller ID. "Hi Dani. Did Luke arrive safely?"

"Yes, he's here and ready to come to your place whenever you're ready. It doesn't have to be today, I know you're busy."

"Today is fine. I'm looking forward to it. Give me an hour to finish up a few things here at the bar and then I'll head home."

It was good to hear her voice. He hadn't given much thought to the last leg of the trip before today. He missed their conversation that last half a day but thought perhaps she was tired. It had been a long two days, although he thought she seemed a bit miffed at him but his intuition about females was not the best, for sure.

"Hey, Boss, before you leave, could you give me Danielle's phone number?" Mitch asked.

Jace hesitated. "Sure, I guess I can, but what do you need it for?"

Mitch smiled, "I want to ask her out. I think she would be a fun date and besides that, she's really pretty. Don't you think so?"

Jace frowned. "Yeah, she is pretty. I'll ask her if it's okay to give you her number when I see her today. I don't want to give it out if she wants to keep it private."

"Sure, I understand. Ask her and if she says yes, I'm going to ask her to go to the movies on Saturday night."

'Why is this bothering you so much, Jace? You have no exclusive rights to Dani's friendship. Mitch is a perfect person to ask her out and you know he'd be a gentleman. And if he wasn't, I'm pretty sure Dani could handle him. Besides, you're not her big brother or her father. You're just a friend and maybe not that. She didn't seem to think too highly of your plan to date a wealthy older woman.'

"Are you ready, Luke? I'm not sure what Jace has planned for the two of you today but I'm sure it will be instructive in some way."

They pulled into the drive which curved around to the house and barn. Jace's truck was there so obviously he arrived before them. He came out to meet them, shook hands with Luke and was going to give Dani a handshake too but she kept her hands in the pockets of her jacket.

"It's nice to meet you, Luke. The last time I saw you was the day I bought the two horses from your dad and I believe you were maybe one or two years old. You've grown just a little bit since then."

Luke laughed. At thirteen, he was tall like his dad and was going to have his broad shoulders, too. He had also inherited his mom's red hair, although a much darker shade of red.

"Let's go in the house for a bit and talk about what you'd like to gain from these two weeks in Montana." Looking at Dani, he said, "You're welcome to come in too. That way you won't have to make two trips."

"Thanks for the offer but I have things to do at home and some errands in town. What time do you want me to pick him up? If you still have my phone number, you can text me when he's ready."

"Yes I have it. Speaking of phone numbers…never mind. I was going to ask if you had mine but obviously you do since we spoke this morning."

She nodded and walked back to her truck. Before she got in, she told Luke, "You're too old to tell you to be a good boy, so I'll just remind you to do what your parents would want. Okay?" With that she drove off.

'Why didn't you ask if it was okay to give Mitch her number, Jace? Admit it…you really don't want him to call her.'

He grabbed two bottles of water from the refrigerator and they sat at the kitchen table.

"Your grandpa Cal tells me you've wanted to be a rodeo man since you could talk and walk, Luke."

"Yes, sir, I have. I never wanted to be a rancher."

"Why do you think that's true? What intrigues you about the rodeo? I'm sure you've been to the rodeos in Houston, right?"

Luke nodded. "Yes sir, I have and I wanted to be in the ring instead of the bleachers."

Jace smiled. "First, let's get something out of the way. I appreciate that your parents have taught you respect for your elders but let's forget the 'sir' for the next two weeks and you just call me Jace, like my friends do, okay? Because we are friends already and I have no doubt we'll be better friends by the time you go home, Luke."

"Okay, sir...I mean, Jace."

They spent much of the morning discussing the positives of rodeo life. Luke sounded so much like him when he was young; he hated to squash all his dreams on the first day by talking trash about the rodeos. He showed him his many pictures and the trophies he'd won. There were newspaper clippings and even articles in national magazines about his skills. Luke's eyes got bigger and his grin got wider. He was impressed. That's what Jace was trying to achieve because if he started on the pinnacle of his success it would be easier to work his way down to the bottom.

"It was a great life for a single guy, Luke, for quite a few years. But I wouldn't be truthful if I didn't tell you the other side of the story, too. I can only speak for myself but I know what I tell you is true of many men and women involved with the rodeo. It seems like the applause and adulation from the stands will last forever, but it doesn't. When the crowds go home, you still have to take care of your animals and your tack, regardless of how tired and banged up you are. Then you have to load it all up and drive to the next site. Some days, you stop long enough to collect your winnings and some days, there are no winnings."

They continued talking until Jace thought that was enough for one day. They went to the barn and Luke showed him his roping skills with a makeshift wooden calf Jace had pulled out of the back of the barn. Jace had to admit the kid was darned good for a thirteen year old.

* * *

"Did Jace already leave?" Mitch asked Maggie.

"Yep. Said he was going to talk to a kid about not joining the rodeo. Why?"

"I asked him for Danielle's phone number but he didn't give it to me yet."

"I think I have it," Maggie told him. "The first day she came in here looking for Jace, she gave it to me. I threw it in the drawer. Wait a minute."

A few minutes later, she retrieved the slip of paper and handed it to him. "Here ya go, Mitch. Good luck. I hope she says she'll go out with you. That is what you wanted it for, right?"

He took the paper and ignored her remark.

CHAPTER 23

CAMILLE DECIDED TO work from a nearby coffee house for a change of scenery. She took her laptop and was working diligently on responding to the 'hellos' on the site with the younger men. She scrolled through the profile pictures, responded to some and dismissed others. She was suddenly surprised to see one of the same faces she'd seen on the senior site. What was up with this guy named Antonio? Did he join every site? She already had his email address so she contacted him. He remembered her and they resumed their online friendship where they'd left it. She was certain his ultimate goal was to meet for a one night stand but she was willing to see how far the conversations would go before it reached that point.

When she agreed to do the six month series, she promised herself she would be truthful with her readers...up to a point. She would fictionalize any sexual encounters as she had no desire to be with a different man every few weeks or, heaven forbid, to actually fall for someone. That would be a bit of a mess. *'Yes, I really am falling in love with you but wait...my name isn't Emily, I don't live in Montana and everything about me is a lie.'*

She kept a hard copy log of every man she spoke with or emailed or met. She needed those notes to put into each month's submission. So far, she had met several of them in person. She made sure they met during the day for lunch or coffee in a safe place with lots of people present. She realized she had inadvertently left her log at home so she scribbled notes on a pad of paper she had in her purse. She would decipher them when she got home.

The first man was at least twenty years older than he claimed to be. The second one had some strange beliefs, at least in her opinion. The subject of owning a gun was discussed. He was mortified that she would even entertain that idea. She assured him she didn't own one and had no plans to purchase one but she understood why many women did. He strongly disapproved of harming anything...ants, flies, mosquitoes...rodents. Growing weary of his continued belaboring the point, she asked, "So if a mouse ran across your kitchen counter, you wouldn't set a trap? Or if a mosquito was biting you, you wouldn't kill it?" He shook his head, "Absolutely not."

Yesterday, she met the third man. He was dressed in a suit and seemed very business-like. They had nearly finished their lunch when he suddenly told her he had to leave because his mother was calling him. He promptly stood up and walked out.

She should be able to write a good column for next month, for sure. Did she attract wackos or what? Where were all the men who were simply looking for a date or maybe a relationship? One thing she could definitely tell her readers...do not believe much of anything you read in a man's profile.

She checked her watch and realized she'd told Collier she needed him to fix the desk she was using. The leg was loose and it wobbled, annoyingly, when she was trying to work. He knew the code for the keypad so he could let himself in if she didn't make it home in time.

*   *   *

Collier knocked several times but there was no response. Obviously, Camille wasn't home. She'd told him to use the code if she wasn't there so he did. He would have to remove her papers from the desk in order to fix it. He carefully picked up each pile and placed it on the table by the desk. As he moved the last pile to the table, he couldn't help but glance at the long list of names...all men's names and their ages. His eyes couldn't stop reading the notes about each one.

What the heck was this and who was Camille aka Emily? He felt bad about seeing the lists but he had a suspicion she hadn't come to Montana to write a novel. Unless, of course, it had fifty male characters in it.

When Camille entered the house, there was a note on the kitchen counter saying Collier had been there and the desk was fixed. She checked the time, hoping she had a few hours to compose more notes and transfer the ones she wrote at the coffee shop. As she sat at her desk, the thought struck her that Collier had to see the lists of men's names she wrote on a legal pad. That realization made her feel terrible and at the same time, made her laugh. She could only imagine what Collier was thinking.

She finished putting her thoughts on paper. She hurried to take a shower and prepare to meet one more man today. He wasn't able to meet during the day but told her to choose a place she felt comfortable since it would be evening. Perhaps this was a guy who was actually okay. She only knew of one place to meet where she had been before and that was *The Branding Iron*.

* * *

Camille's stomach was growling and she didn't want to consume much more alcohol on an empty stomach but she was growing impatient as her 'date' hadn't appeared yet and it was an hour after the specified time. She was going to order.

If he showed up now, he'd better have a darned good excuse. As she perused the menu, she was aware of a man approaching her table.

"Emily? What are you doing in here all alone?"

She glanced up and was looking at that sexy smile again. It was Jace, the man she met the night Collier brought her here. She shook her head and motioned for him to pull up a chair.

"Well, it's like this...I've been stood up and I'm not too happy about it," she explained.

"I can't imagine any man being stupid enough to stand you up," was his reply.

"Can I hug you here in front of your customers?" she laughingly asked him. "That's the nicest thing I've heard today."

She ordered a sandwich and they talked while she ate. She briefly explained she was supposed to meet someone for dinner but that was now almost two hours ago. He told her about having his name on a dating site and the same thing had happened to him the week before. They continued chatting and laughing about the horrors of dating when you weren't a teen any longer.

Camille glanced around the room and realized there weren't many customers. Her eyes landed on a man leaning on the bar and she thought he looked familiar, even with his back to her.

She covered her mouth to keep from screaming. She grabbed Jace's arm and whispered, "Is there a back way out of here? Please say there is."

He saw the anger in her face and followed her gaze to the man at the bar. He quietly took her arm and placed his body between her and the man so he wouldn't be able to see her even if he turned around. Then he quietly guided her to his office in the back and closed the door.

She sat down and her face was ashen. "How in the world did that son of a bitch find me?"

"Who is he and why are you frightened? Do you want me to ask him to leave?"

"His name is Will and I'm not actually frightened by him…I'm just unbelievably ticked off. He's someone from my past and he's not supposed to know where I am. In a town this size, what are the odds he'd end up at this bar on the same night I'm here? He's supposed to be in St. Louis."

"We can wait until he's gone or we can go out the back door but either way, I'll drive you home, Emily."

"Thank you but that won't be necessary."

"I'd feel much better if I took you home. I'll pick you up tomorrow and bring you back to get your car. I insist."

*   *   *

In the morning, Maggie opened the doors at *The Branding Iron* and found Jace already there.

"You're an early bird today. Got your chores done early or couldn't sleep again last night? Give me a minute and I'll have the coffee ready."

"I'm going to need something stronger than coffee, Maggie."

She tilted her head to one side and gave him a questioning look. He rarely drank much at all and certainly not in the morning.

"What's up, Boss Man?"

"I don't even know how to put this into words, Maggie. Just the thought of it tears me up inside."

There was no point in sugar coating the words or stalling. "I'm going to have to let you go. You know it isn't because I want to. You are and always will be the best bartender in the entire state of Montana but I can't afford to pay you any longer. You're not making what you're worth now and things haven't gotten much better around here. There has been a bit of increase in our receipts but not enough. I'm thinking I'll have to put *The Branding Iron* on the market and I know Blakeley is going to swoop in and buy it."

She came around to his side of the bar and put her arms around his neck. "Listen, Jace, I've seen this coming for quite a while now and I've been saving for this day. You can't get rid of me that easy. Let's give it a few more months and see what happens. Maybe business will continue to pick up. I'll live on my tips and you don't have to pay me…unless…"

That made him laugh. "You never give up, do you? You're going to try to convince me to sleep with you, one way or the other. I don't think I can claim that as a legitimate expense on my taxes."

Maggie stood and started to make the big pot of coffee for the regular crowd. "There is one stipulation and it has nothing to do with sex. No one else can know I'm not receiving a paycheck, agreed?"

He nodded his head. "Agreed. But I will continue to keep record of your hours and if this crisis is ever over or if I sell the place, you will be the first person I pay."

The regulars were beginning to straggle in for their morning cup of coffee.

"Hey, look, fellas. Either we're late or Jace is early. Couldn't sleep last night, Cowboy?"

Jace shook his head and grinned. "I slept just fine."

"I'll bet you did after spending time with that purty woman Collier brought in a few nights ago. Does he know you're steppin' on his toes with her?"

"We only met here by chance last night. How do you old gossips know that already?"

They all laughed. "Haven't you figured out by now we know everything that goes on in this town?"

Ralph added, "We know you took her home, too. I guess you're finally taking our advice, huh? Date an older woman with money and ask her to invest in *The Branding Iron*. I think you found your cougar, for sure.

"Slow down and back up. Who says she has money and no, we're not dating."

"Come on, Jace. She lives on Flagler Rd. Everybody living there has money and lots of it."

"Believe what you want. I have to get home. I'm teaching a young kid about the rodeo."

Chapter 24

DANI'S CELL PHONE beeped but she didn't recognize the number. She answered cautiously.

"Hello?"

"Hi Danielle. This is Mitch. I work at *The Branding Iron* and I brought you and Jace water and fruit the first day you were in there and I wondered if you're not busy if you might want to go to the movies with me on Friday night. I know it's kind of short notice but I didn't have your phone number and Jace left without giving it to me but Maggie still had it and that's my only night off."

Dani had to laugh. Mitch didn't take a breath anywhere in those sentences and she was pretty sure that would win a prize as the longest 'asking for a date' in history. She made a quick decision to accept and simply said, "Yes."

There was a rather long pause and then she heard him say, "Really? I mean…great, great! Is there a particular film you'd like to see?"

"I'll let you choose, Mitch. I like most any kind except total blood and gore."

"Okay. Would you like to have a bite to eat before? I can pick you up around five if that works for you."

She assured him that would be perfect before she remembered she was supposed to pick Luke up from Jace's house at 6:30.

She called Jace. "I don't think Luke will be able to come to your house on Friday afternoon. I've made plans and won't be able to pick him up and Dad doesn't drive any longer."

"It's okay, Dani. He can still come over. We don't have too much longer to work together so I hate to skip a day. What do you say to allowing him to stay the night? I'm not a prize-winning chef but I won't let him starve. Then he'll be here fresh and early on Saturday morning and I'll bring him home around noon because I'll have to be at the bar on Saturday evening."

She had several thoughts go through her head in rapid succession. There were so many horrible stories out there about men and young boys and she had been entrusted with Luke's safety. How well did she really know Jace? *'You crawled in bed with him and trusted him, Silly.'* That was a true statement even if she said it in her head. "Yes, that will be fine, if Luke is okay with it. I'll talk to him and let you know."

Later that afternoon Cal called to see how things were going.

"Is Luke behaving himself?"

"You know you don't even have to ask that question, Calvin Frasier," Dani told him. She handed the phone to Luke so he and Cal, and Lucy who was listening on speaker, could talk for a while. Luke described the activities Jace had him doing. He also talked about all the trophies Jace had won. Cal wasn't so sure that would lead to the outcome they'd hoped for but maybe Jace had a plan.

"We're happy to hear things are going well, Luke. Put Dani back on the phone, will you?"

"Do you have a phone number where I can reach Jace? I had it but obviously, I lost it. I want to talk to him about what I think is a terrific idea but I don't know how he'll feel about it."

She gave him Jace's personal number and the number at *The Branding Iron*. After some goodbyes, they ended the conversation.

*   *   *

Jace answered his phone when he recognized Cal Frasier's name. He assumed Cal was calling to inquire about Luke and how things were going. Instead, Cal said, "Hey Jace, Lucy and I have a favor to ask of you and your bar."

"Okay, shoot," Jace said, a bit bewildered. He couldn't imagine what *The Branding Iron* could do for them.

"It's a bit complicated. Remember the band we told you about and you accused us of being their 'groupies,'? The Hubie Ashcraft Band, from Indiana," he said hoping to refresh Jace's memory. "Anyway, they've had a monkey wrench thrown in their plans and Lucy and I thought maybe you could help them out."

"I will if I can, Cal."

"They've been in Seattle for a music festival and played several gigs here. The original plan was to make their way back to Indiana with stops along the way. They were contracted to play in Great Falls, Montana for two weekends before they worked their way to Minneapolis and then Chicago on their way home. Hubie told me he received a call yesterday from the venue in Great Falls. Due to some difficulties he didn't share with me, they won't be able to play there. That means a long drive and wasted time getting back home. I told him I would speak to you and see if you'd be interested in having them play at your bar. Bozeman would be almost on their path home. If you don't have any other groups scheduled, of course."

Jace couldn't think of anything to say but his mind was working overtime. This could be an answer to prayers...which he hadn't said...having great entertainment for a few weekends would bring in paying customers, many who had never been there before and probably didn't know *The Branding Iron* even existed. Ken would be thrilled that his plan was going to come to fruition. But how in the world would he pay them? He'd have to pass up the opportunity as awesome as it was. He didn't have the money and that was all there was to it.

"Cal, you caught me off guard, a little. Can you give me a day or two to think about it? Don't misunderstand…I would be thrilled to have them perform here. I'll need to check schedules and a few other things before I commit, okay?"

"Of course, of course. That's not the kind of decision you can make in a few minutes…especially since I sprung it on you out of the blue so to speak. Give me a call when you decide, one way or the other."

*   *   *

He had a million thoughts running through his head as he drove to Emily's house to bring her back to pick up her car. That whole incident last night was bizarre too. She said she wasn't afraid of this Will guy but she certainly didn't want to see him. She hadn't elaborated much when he drove her home. He did go inside to make sure everything was okay before he left her there alone. Ken was probably right about the fact she had money. It was quite the house…bigger than any of the other 'mansions' on Flagler Rd. She could turn it into a lodge and have it filled to capacity every week, probably. What did one person need with that many rooms? He didn't know and it wasn't any of his business.

"Hi Jace," she greeted him when he rang the bell. "Come in for a minute. Have a seat. I have to finish one small thing before I can leave. There's water or juice in the refrigerator if you want some," she said from the den or office or whatever room she disappeared into.

He grabbed a bottle of water and stood at the counter, looking around again at his surroundings. The kitchen was bigger than the one at the bar, he realized. He turned to look out the window and admire the view she could see every day as she cooked or made coffee or whatever… He saw Collier's truck come down the street with the turn signal on indicating he was turning into Emily's drive but suddenly he sped past instead. That was strange. He could have stopped and said hello. He certainly would have recognized Jace's truck.

Just then, Emily appeared, looking as good as she had the night before. "Okay, I'm ready. I'm sorry you had to wait. I had something I had to get sent."

They talked about a lot of things on the way back into town but 'Will' wasn't one of them. Before she got out of his truck and prepared to get into her car, he asked if she would consider going out with him some night.

"I'll make sure I take you somewhere other than here," he laughed as he nodded toward his bar.

She accepted his invitation and they chose Saturday evening.

CHAPTER 25

WILL REACHED BETWEEN his feet and rummaged around in his carry-on bag, looking for the latest copy of *Mavis' Mag* he purchased before he left St Louis. When he bought it, he thought perhaps there might be some clues to Camille's whereabouts. He made plans to have a short stopover in Bozeman since he was smugly sure his deductions had been correct and he would find her. Now he was on his way to California and still had not located Camille. He knew when he made the reservations that he was probably playing a long shot. Bozeman wasn't a little burg but a thriving community with enough restaurants and bars to keep him busy searching for months, instead of hours.

He made some inquiries of waitresses and bartenders asking if any of them recognized her name but it was a hopeless cause. If her picture had been on the inside page like it always was in the past, he could've asked if anyone had seen her but she was smart…he'd give her that. With no photo in the magazine, there was no chance of anyone recognizing her.

Now it seemed his search for his magazine was a hopeless cause too. He had it with him last night so he must have left it in one of the places he looked for her. He rested his head against the back of his seat. His long legs were always cramped on planes these days. When he worked for the brokerage house, he flew first class and didn't have that problem.

Thinking about his previous employer took his mind back to the papers he wanted from Camille's safe. Somewhere between stewing about them and listening to Lorna's pleas for him to come to the west coast, he had a revelation: in all probability, those papers weren't in the safe any longer. Camille was paranoid enough or vindictive enough that she probably took them with her, knowing she was going to be gone for six months. That was when he made the decision to go and see what Lorna had for him in the way of employment opportunities.

*   *   *

Jace flipped the burgers he had on the grill for him and Luke. "Grab the slices of cheese and the buns, Luke. We'll take these inside or we'll be eating in the dark."

He hadn't meant for supper to be so late. They had a good afternoon. Luke helped him uncover an old mechanical bull he had buried under a lot of unused things in the back of the barn. Many years ago, Jace took a group of wealthy cattle buyers on a guided fishing trip. One of the men had it sent to Jace as a joke after he returned home. At the time, it seemed like a slap in the face considering the man knew Jace could no longer participate in the rodeos like he used to.

He'd tried to sell it but there wasn't much interest so it was stored away where he wouldn't have to look at it and be reminded of his former life. Truthfully, he forgot all about it until a few days ago. Surprisingly, with a bit of WD-40 and some minor adjustments, it still worked. He spent the afternoon giving Luke all the tips he could recall about staying astride a bucking bull.

"You're gonna sleep good tonight, Luke," he told him.

Luke nodded and tried to grin but his mouth was full of cheeseburger.

"Dani says I sleep like a log and I snore so she'll be happy I had to spend the night here," Luke told him.

"Speaking of Dani, she said she was busy tonight. Do you know where she went?" Jace asked him.

Luke nodded. "Yep. She had a date for dinner and a movie with some guy named Mitch."

Jace nearly choked on his sandwich. *'How did Mitch get her number? I didn't give it to him. What do I care? She can date whoever she wants. It's none of my business.'*

After they cleaned up the few dishes, they sat in the living room and talked. "I thought you'd probably have a video game or two with you. Do you play them at home?"

"Yes, but we're only allowed to play for a few hours each day. My mom says she doesn't want our brains to turn to mush." They both laughed at that.

"It sounds like you have a wonderful family, Luke."

"Yeah, I guess so. There are a lot of us but since Grandpa Cal and Grams gave us the whole ranch house, it isn't cramped any longer. They built a new one for themselves."

Jace vaguely remembered the Frasier ranch house and it seemed huge to him at the time.

"You're very lucky to have all those siblings. I always wanted a brother but never had one."

Luke seemed amazed by that. "You don't have any brothers or sisters? You have other relatives, though, right?"

Jace shook his head. "Nope. Well, I have a mother somewhere but I don't know her."

Luke seemed confused. "I can't imagine life without my mom and dad. What happened to yours?"

Jace stretched his long legs out in front of him and told him his life story, in condensed form. "My Grandpa Matthews came to Bozeman many years ago. He had two sons: my dad and my Uncle Henry. Grandpa bought 160 acres bordering BLM land…that's government land that you can use but can't build on. When his sons grew up, he gave each one a parcel of eighty acres. My dad married and they had me but one day, when I was still little, my mom packed a bag and left and never came back. When I was a teenager, my dad remarried but his new wife and I never got along too well. That's when I decided I was going to leave. I didn't want to join the circus so the rodeo was the next best thing." He grinned so Luke would realize he was kidding about the circus.

"On one of my visits back home, Dad said he was selling the eighty acres because his new wife didn't like living in the 'middle of nowhere' as she called Bozeman."

My Uncle Henry never married and therefore had no children. When he died, I inherited his eighty acres which I mortgaged to put a down payment on *The Branding Iron*. I thought I was set for life. It didn't work out that way, though."

"My dad would say God had other plans for your life," Luke interjected.

Jace frowned a bit. "Yeah, you could say that, I guess."

"So what happened? How come you stopped being with the rodeos?"

"I was in an accident that could have been prevented but someone didn't do their job. The gate opened unexpectedly, I wasn't prepared like I should have been and I was trampled by the biggest bull on the circuit. I spent months in the hospital and longer in rehab. They told me my leg and hip were broken in so many pieces, repairing it was like putting a jigsaw puzzle together. At first they told me I'd never walk again but I worked hard and I did. As you can see, I have a noticeable limp I'll never overcome and some days it hurts more than others but at least I can walk."

"I had insurance on my belongings but foolishly, I never had any insurance on my body. It took all the money I had saved to pay the hospital bills. When I came back here, I decided to become a guide for fishermen and hunters and for people who wanted to experience a week in the wilderness. I made enough money at that too but the longer I did it and the older I got, the more I realized I couldn't ride long enough at one time to be able to do that any longer."

"I'm really sorry that happened to you, Jace. I suppose my parents thought if you told me that, I'd stop wanting to follow my dream."

"I don't believe they want to squash your dreams, Luke and neither do I. The possibility of being hurt is present with any occupation. You could get trampled being a rancher, too. If I was going to tell you something to sway your thinking, it would be about loneliness, not about broken bones. I always thought someday I would have a wife and a couple of kids I loved. You know, a family like yours back home in Texas. But that's something you'll have to think real hard about because it isn't fair to be gone all the time and leave them alone. If you want to make the rodeo your occupation and not a weekend hobby, you will be gone all the time. You'll never see your kids' ballgames or piano recitals or any of those things because you have to move on to the next town to make some more money. Do you understand what I'm saying?"

"Yes sir," Luke answered.

"Lets' have some ice cream. I think I've talked enough for one night."

As they ate their sundaes with all the fixins' Luke said, "Can I ask you something?"

"Absolutely. Ask anything."

"Do you believe in God? I mean, I heard you say the other day that you didn't pray anymore and you seemed a bit upset when I talked about God's plan for your life, so I just wondered."

"Honestly, I don't know the answer to that. I did believe in God when I was your age and when I was a young adult. I went to Sunday School when I was a kid, learned the Bible stories and said my prayers about everything."

"What happened to make you stop believing?"

"I prayed about a lot of things, Luke. I prayed my mom would come back, then after I got hurt, I asked God to let me walk normal again. It seemed God wasn't listening so I stopped asking."

"God always hears our prayers but sometimes, he chooses a different answer than the one we're asking for. You said you never gave up when you wanted to walk again so why did you give up so easily when you didn't get what you wanted from God?"

Jace had no answer but he told Luke, "I think you should forget about the rodeo, Son, and become an evangelist instead."

CHAPTER 26

CAMILLE CHECKED HER image in the mirror and nodded. She thought she looked put together for her first official date with Jace. She had chosen a dress with red accents which seemed to be begging for her red heels. She had grown fond of the *jeans and boots* look but tonight she would show him another side of her. She tapped her foot on the floor until she realized she was doing it again. *'What are you nervous about? Just because he's a particularly handsome man who also happens to be fourteen years younger than you...why should that make you nervous?'* She laughed at her thoughts. She was nervous but this is what she wanted to write the column about. This is what she came here for. Maybe they didn't meet online but the readers would assume they had. The same concerns about the age difference were there regardless of where they met.

He was right on time and looked good enough to eat. That was an old saying and she had to remember tonight not to say things that would age her. This could be an interesting night but she was ready for it. *'Bring it on, Jace Matthews.'*

He took her to a nice restaurant in a newer part of town. She asked him to explain the Old Bozeman and New Bozeman concept Collier had mentioned. Jace said basically the same thing Collier had. There were some people who resented any changes, even good ones but for the most part, everyone got along and they had one thing in common. They all loved the town and Montana...well, almost all of them. He described Blakely, who didn't love anything but money.

"You wouldn't sell him the bar, would you?"

"Not if I can help it, I won't." Jace told her about Cal's offer to have a band for two consecutive weekends.

"I haven't given him my answer yet. I'd like nothing better and I believe with the right amount of advertising, it might just be the answer to my prayers." *'Really, Jace? When did you pray about it?'*

"So, what's stopping you? Go for it. Tell your friend to tell the band to 'come on down' or 'come on over' I guess would be the right term if I know my geography."

"Truthfully, I don't have the kind of money it would take to pay them. The second weekend I might be able to pay with the first weekend receipts but I can't afford the initial payment."

"That's unfortunate. I want your bar to succeed and I definitely don't want anyone to buy it out from under you. How about a loan?"

"I don't think the bank is going to consider me a good risk."

"Sort of like throwing good money after bad, huh?" *'You just did it again, Camille. He's probably never heard that saying. Stop it!'*

"Actually, I meant I would loan you the money, Jace."

"I couldn't let you do that, Emily. You don't even know me. We've just met and...no, no, that wouldn't work."

"Sure it would. I have it and you need it. It's as simple as that. If it makes you feel any better, we could write something up but I'm good with just a handshake, if you are."

"Let me think about it until tomorrow. I don't feel right about it."

"Please don't tell me you have some antiquated notion that says you can't take money from a woman. I'll bet you'd jump on the offer if it came from a man."

"Guilty as charged," he told her.

They continued their discussion of many topics and ended the evening with a walk around some of the picturesque streets. He took her home and walked her to the door.

"Would you like to come in for a minute? I have wine, beer or soft drinks. What's your pleasure?"

"I'll take a beer and then I have to go. Chores to do in the morning."

He toyed with the drops on the outside of his glass for a while and then asked, "Emily, can you tell me about the man in the bar last night? I don't want to pry but he certainly irritated you and despite what you said to the contrary, I believe he frightened you, too. At least, a little."

She took a swallow of wine and started to tell him a few things about Will. "I was married to him once upon a time, Jace. Many years ago. We were both in college although I graduated before him...I'm six years older than him." She smiled a rather seductive smile, pulled him to his feet and said, "I guess I've always been attracted to younger men."

He put his arms around her and pulled her to him. She smelled wonderful but the scent was light, not overpowering. She felt good in his arms and her lips were soft and warm when he kissed her. *'Maybe you haven't forgotten what it's like to hold a woman, Jace.'*

When he finally left, he had agreed to her offer of a loan for the band. They sealed the deal with more than a handshake but less than spending the night together.

'What the hell just happened, Jace? You have never even kissed a woman on a first date and you just about did a whole lot more than that on this first date. And why did Dani's face keep appearing in your thoughts?'

* * *

When he rolled out of bed the next morning, he pinched himself to see if he was awake or dreaming and asked himself if he dreamed the entire date last night. Evidently not, because there were a few lipstick smudges on the collar of his shirt which he'd thrown on a chair.

'Between Luke preaching to me and Emily wanting to loan me the money and then...this has been the most bizarre weekend I've had for a long time.' If he was honest, maybe it was also the most enjoyable.

He did the chores and then called Cal. It went straight to voicemail but they were probably in church at this time of the morning. He would call later and firm up the arrangements for the band to come. In the morning, he would ask the regulars to put their actions where their mouths were and start advertising the upcoming weekends, once he found out exactly when they would be there.

*   *   *

Collier knocked on Camille's door. It was a few minutes before she answered.

"Well, you're up early on a Sunday morning. I haven't even had my coffee yet. Come in, sit down and I'll get you a cup too."

He watched her move around the kitchen, making the coffee. She still had her lightweight pajamas on and they left little to the imagination, for sure. He was having trouble corralling his thoughts while he watched her.

She set his cup down in front of him. "If I remember correctly, you like it black...yes?"

He nodded. "Camille or Emily or whoever you are...I need to talk to you."

"That sounds serious, Collier or maybe ominous. What's going on?"

"That's what I came to ask you. Who are you really and what are you doing in Bozeman? Why don't *you* tell *me* what exactly is going on?"

She fixed him with a look he couldn't quite decipher before she answered. "You already know I'm Barbara's daughter and my real name is Camille. I have a good reason to use the name Emily Hasbro but it isn't illegal to pretend to be someone else for business reasons, is it?"

"Not illegal, I guess but not honest either. I know you left the bar with Jace the other night and he came back to get you the next morning. I saw his truck in your drive. What was that all about?"

'That sounds like a jealous statement, Collier.' Camille took a deep breath and exhaled slowly. "I went to *The Branding Iron* to meet a date but he stood me up. Jace came over to talk for a bit and I saw Will…remember him? He was standing at the bar with his back to me and I asked Jace to get me out of there. He brought me home and in the morning, he came back to get me to take me to my car. End of story."

Collier was looking at her trying to decide if he believed her or not. "Why is Will in town?"

"I wish I knew. If I had to guess, I would say he figured out where I am and was checking different places to see if anyone recognized my name. Fortunately, you're the only one in this town who knows my real name."

"Look, Camille, I care about you. Don't ask me how that's even possible since we hardly know each other, but it's true anyway. I'm worried about you living in this big house all alone. Tell me the truth about why you're here and what's up with all the men's names on the legal pad on your desk. Yes, I saw it. I wasn't snooping but you left it in plain sight when you knew I was coming to fix your desk."

She decided to take a chance and tell him the truth, at least some of it…but not all of it. It would be better if he didn't know the nature of the articles she was writing considering he might be the subject of one in the future.

Several cups of coffee later, he stood and went to her side of the table. He bent down and kissed her. Then he left without saying a word.

Camille hurried to her computer and wrote furiously about last night's evening with Jace and this morning with Collier. She didn't want to forget a thing as it would make the article so much better with all the details included. She enhanced the facts about her time with Jace and made the love scene as realistic as possible without totally offending her readers.

CHAPTER 27

CAL AND JACE spoke and finalized the dates for the band to be at *The Branding Iron*. Jace made sure he was present when the table of regulars was full.

"Okay, you guys...here's the deal. You've been spouting ideas for saving this bar for months. While I appreciate all the suggestions, it seems Ken had the best idea when he said we should have some entertainment that would draw a crowd. We have an opportunity to make that happen but here's where you come in. Between all of you, you seem to know everyone in this town and the surrounding area. I need your help to get the word out...everywhere you can think of. I'll have some flyers made to place in the shops but if you have any connections with businesses, ask if they'll put the information on their outdoor signs. In the end, word of mouth is still the best advertisement. I'm getting a copy of one of their CDs in the mail and I'll make sure it gets played in here...a lot."

"Oh and one more thing...if you have any legitimate ideas for the first night crowd, I'd like to hear them, too. I'm counting on that first crowd to tell their friends and bring them back."

"That's great news, Jace but what happens when this band is gone? What then?"

"I asked myself that same question, Ralph. I'm praying our new customers' experiences at *The Branding Iron* will be so impressive, they'll want to come back and tell their friends about the food, the atmosphere and the beautiful and talented bartender, Miss Maggie." He grinned at her over his shoulder. She threw the bar rag she was holding at his head.

'Jace, that's the third or fourth time you've said you'd be praying about something. Did Luke's words get to you?'

Ken's smile was spreading across his face. "You did it, didn't you? You rascal…I didn't think you had enough time or enough dates with the lady to ask for money, but you must be even smoother than I thought you were. And in honor of your obvious exceptional prowess with the lady, you can advertise a free drink for the first 100 customers, which I will gladly pay for."

Jace realized Ken was sure he'd slept with Emily to get the money and sometime in the future he'd tell him the truth but Ken wouldn't believe him now, anyway.

Not to be outdone by Ken, one of the men offered to pay for an advertising spot on the radio and another said he would handle the cost of placing an ad in the newspaper.

They really were his good friends and Jace was thanking God for them. *'Stop it Jace. You just did it again..by Sunday, you'll be preaching at the local church.'*

"Maggie, do you think any of your nieces or nephews would like a job for a few days in the afternoon? I'd like this place to be spic and span clean before our big weekend."

* * *

Later in the day, when the morning coffee-drinkers were gone, Maggie asked, "So tell me, Boss Man, did you really sleep with the woman named Emily on your first date? I'm happy for you if you did but I must admit, after all my failed efforts to get you in the sack, I'm quite jealous."

Dani had just entered the bar and overheard Maggie's question. She interrupted and told Jace that Luke was outside waiting for him. She didn't want to stick around to hear any more about Jace and one of his online dating conquests.

"Wait, Dani," he said as he chased her down. "Please don't believe what you just heard. It's not true. You know how they all like to tease me."

She nodded slightly. "Luke is in your truck waiting for you like we arranged. I have errands to do. I'll see you later."

She drove off and he knew she didn't believe him.

* * *

The rest of the afternoon was spent with Luke. Jace's dog Jake loved Luke and followed him everywhere. That surprised Jace a little as Jake didn't always accept people immediately. Obviously, he could sense that Luke was a good kid.

When they took a break, Luke was throwing sticks for Jake and Jace was resting with a glass of lemonade in his hand. He watched the dog/boy interaction and realized he longed for a family like Ben Frasier had...a houseful of kids, a wife who loved him and was there for him. Those were things he never experienced as a child or adult and he didn't really expect, at this age, to have any of it come true. He resigned himself to taking his happiness where he found it and he was pretty happy in Emily's arms the other night. He was taking her out again. He'd always felt like he was older than his years so he was comfortable with their age difference. She was very attractive, fun to be with and a good conversationalist. What more could a man ask for? *'Are you positive her being wealthy doesn't add to her charm?'*

He dismissed the thought as fast as it surfaced. He enjoyed her company, plain and simple and if that led to more intimate things...he was ready for that, too.

*   *   *

Collier arrived at Camille's house to fix some outdoor gutters that had been damaged by the winter's snows. He was on a ladder when Camille came out. She shaded her eyes with her hand and squinted up at him.

"I have some lunch ready if you'd like to come in and eat with me. Don't get too excited…it's only egg salad on rye."

This woman was going to drive him to drink. She looked good in anything. Today, she had on a pair of cut-off shorts and a t-shirt. Pretty simple but she made it look like a fashion statement. He couldn't keep his eyes off her when they were together.

"Would you like to go to dinner this evening?"

"I would but I have other plans. I'm sorry. Could we do it tomorrow night?"

"Sure. Tomorrow's good." *'I wonder if tonight's plans include Jace Matthews.'*

Her phone beeped. She glanced at the number and frowned. "It's a call from Paris, France. Guess who that might be. Barbara's probably checking up on me…asking if I've broken any of her precious possessions yet."

Collier asked, "Aren't you going to answer it? Maybe it's important."

"I'll call her back later…or never. Nothing she could possibly want is important to me."

He shrugged his shoulders, indicating her and Barbara's relationship was none of his business and he planned on keeping his nose out of it.

"Tell me, Camille, when we go somewhere together, does our age difference bother you?"

"Since I'm the older one…the cougar as they call it…I think I should be asking that question of you."

"We're only ten years apart and I'm very comfortable with that so I don't think it will ever be a problem for me."

"That's good to know, Collier because I'd like to continue to see you."

*   *   *

"Where we goin' Jace?" Luke asked when they got in the truck after loading Jesse in the trailer.

"We're on our way to a friend's house who has a few calves in a pasture. Jesse hasn't done any calf-roping work for a few years but you're an experienced rider so you shouldn't have any trouble. I don't want you to throw the calves or tie their legs. I want to see how well you do at riding full speed and throwing a rope over their neck. By the time you go home, we should have covered most of the rodeo events, even though you're obviously not going to choose to become proficient at more than one."

Jace delivered Luke home in the late afternoon. Dani laughed when she saw him. "Wow. That must have been some workout today. You look like you've been 'rode hard and put away wet' as the saying goes."

Luke nodded. "It was great but I'm gonna take a shower and maybe go to bed before supper. I'm whipped. Oh yeah, Jace said hello. He probably would've come in but I think he has a date. He said he was going home to take a shower and get dressed."

Dani pushed the door shut just a little too hard. "Something botherin' you, Danielle?" her father asked with a slight grin.

"Nope, not a thing, Dad," was her terse response.

Chapter 28

THEY HAD FINISHED their dinner and were contemplating dessert when Emily handed Jace an envelope. He opened it and found a blank check inside.

"I had no idea how much the band charges for two nights so I signed it and left it blank. You can fill it in when you find out. I assume it will be for their lodging and meals also."

"You're awfully trusting for someone who hasn't known me long, Emily. I could put an exorbitant amount in here and fly to Paris or somewhere."

Emily laughed at the reference to Paris. "Go ahead. While you're there would you say hello to my mother?"

When she saw the confused look, she simply said, "That's where she lives, Jace."

'Okay, Camille, now you're getting your men mixed up. You'll have to take notes about what you've shared with whom or you're going to be in lots of trouble.'

She called the waiter over and ordered champagne. "We need a glass of bubbly to make this deal official, don't you agree?"

He nodded, although champagne wouldn't have been his first choice.

They enjoyed the rest of the evening which ended with attending an outdoor concert for a short time. He took her home and walked her to the door. As much as he hated to say good night, he was as tired as Luke had been.

She persuaded him to come inside for a few minutes. "I would love to stay and play," he told her "but I have to be up at the crack of dawn tomorrow and I'm pretty sure you'd wear me out if I stayed the night, Emily."

She placed her hands on his face and murmured, "I would absolutely wear you out, Jace. At least, I'd give it my best shot. You look pretty strong to me; I think you could handle it, Cowboy."

He'd almost decided to stay, regardless of what time he needed to be up in the morning. She was very convincing in all the right ways but before things became too heated, she backed off and told him he probably should leave if he needed to.

Jace walked to his truck totally confused by her mixed signals. Did she want to continue this or not? He was tired and his brain was running on empty. He went home and fell asleep.

*   *   *

Camille sat at her computer and wrote the latest about her dating life. She liked Jace a lot but not enough to actually have a relationship. She gave him the blank check to explain to her readers how easily they could get sucked in when a man they met and liked needed help…usually monetary help. She wrote about Collier, too but so far, he'd not asked for anything from her. She had to admit that Jace didn't ask…she offered…but for the sake of readership, the article stated he asked for the money. She was only interested in saving her magazine and if she had to write some fiction, that was okay, too. *'Is fiction the new term for outright lying, Camille?'* She shushed her inner thoughts by telling herself, the end justified the means.

*   *   *

She spent the next morning contacting and emailing a few men who were new to the dating site. As she flipped through their pictures and profiles, she was surprised to see a man she knew from Missouri. The profile said he now lived in Montana. That was something the team had not anticipated. It was believed the stipulation that all contacts be within a one-hundred mile radius would eliminate the chance anyone she knew would see her picture. Granted, the name was Emily Hasbro but if he recognized her photo…that could be disastrous. *'Oh man, nothing is ever easy. And it was all going so smoothly.'* Maybe he wouldn't contact her.

*   *   *

Cal and Lucy arrived on Saturday. Luke could hardly wait to show them what he'd learned. They accompanied him and Dani to Jace's place, although Dani had been hesitant, saying she'd already heard what they did every day when Luke got home. Lucy convinced her to come along.

When Luke covered all the skills he'd learned in a few weeks, Cal and Lucy were duly impressed. Cal shook Jace's hand. "You've done a good thing for our grandson, Jace. He's a young cowboy, for sure. I've always believed if you're going to try to be the best at something, you should learn from the best and from what Luke tells me, you have enough trophies to prove you were the best."

Jace was humbled by the praise. "It was my pleasure. Luke is an attentive student and an all-around good kid. You can tell your son and daughter-in-law I would hope I had a son like him…if I ever had one. He's taught me a few things too. It was a two-way street."

Lucy hugged Jace. "We're all going to church in the morning, Jace. Won't you please join us?"

Before he could decline their offer, Luke chimed in, "Yeah, and then Dani's fixing dinner. She's a really good cook. Please come along." As an afterthought, he added, "If that's okay with you, Dani."

She shrugged her shoulders. "One more is never a problem, Luke." She looked directly at Jace but was not smiling.

"Please, Jace?" Luke coaxed.

"Okay, you talked me into it. Tell me where I need to be and at what time."

*   *   *

After Jace went home, Luke was talking seriously with his grandparents. He told them something they hadn't expected to hear. "Y'know, I still want to be associated with the rodeo but not for my entire life. Jace told me how lonesome it is and how selfish it would be to marry and have a family but never get to see them. I don't want to do that. I want to have a family like my family back home."

Lucy squeezed Cal's arm until he thought the blood was going to stop flowing. "I think Jace is a very wise man, Luke and I'm glad he shared all aspects of his life and was honest with you."

"Yeah he was honest. I think he's lonesome, too, Grammy. He didn't say that but I could just tell. He's sad he never got to have a family."

"We'll have to pray about that, Luke. He's certainly not too old to start a family now if he finds the right girl..." She wanted to look at Dani but was afraid to. She'd observed the 'not so good' vibes between her and Jace when they were all together earlier.

*   *   *

They discussed the events of the day as they prepared for bed. Cal told Lucy, "We owe Jace a debt of gratitude. No one else has been able to talk Luke into considering something other than full-time rodeo."

"Do you remember when we met for breakfast in Colorado he mentioned in an off-hand way that his bar was in financial trouble? He didn't say it in so many words, but that's what I gathered. How is he going to afford to pay the band and their expenses?" In her typical way, she pronounced, "I think we need to take care of that, Cal...don't you?"

*   *   *

Sunday morning dawned sunny and bright. Luke rolled out amid a chorus of moans and groans. "Oh, man, I am sore," he complained as he stumbled to the kitchen.

"Tell me where it hurts and I'll apply some ointment," Dani's dad told him.

"You'd need a tub full because I hurt everywhere," he proclaimed.

They scurried around, trying to get ready for church. Dani paid special attention to what she chose to wear and her hair. Then she chided herself, *'What do you care, Danielle? It doesn't matter what you wear, you can't compete with the woman he's been seeing. And what difference does it make, anyway?'* She threw her hairbrush in the drawer and went to the truck.

*   *   *

Jace was regretting agreeing to go to church with them but it was too late now to back out. A commitment was a commitment. As he sat in the small church, he felt like he was a kid again. The music, the familiar hymns...they all made him feel as though he'd come home. He wasn't sure if he liked it or not. One thing he knew…he'd be more comfortable if Danielle wasn't giving him looks that said she'd rather push him off a cliff than sit by him in church. Oh, well, he told himself it was only an hour. He could live through anything that only lasted an hour.

He tried to beg off of dinner at Dani's but Luke wouldn't allow him to leave after the service. He had trouble saying no to this young man so he found himself sitting at Dani's dining room table with Cal, Lucy, Luke, Dani and her father, Dean. Luke had been correct. Dani was an excellent cook. He offered to help clear the table and do the dishes while the others visited with Dean, even though Dani protested. They did manage to talk and laugh a little as they struggled to get past each other in her small kitchen. At one point, he reached across her which put her between his arms. For a fleeting moment, as they looked at each other, he had the biggest urge to kiss her but the moment passed.

'Okay, Jace, what the heck are you thinking? Practically sleeping with Emily and wanting desperately to kiss Dani? Are you trying to cram the last years of abstinence into one month or what?'

CHAPTER 29

MAGGIE CHECKED EVERYTHING at the bar. Her niece and two nephews had done a thorough job of making sure every crack and corner was polished and spit-shined, as her daddy used to say. It was as ready as it was going to be. Now she could hardly wait to meet the members of this band that was hopefully going to turn the finances of *The Branding Iron* around. At least, she hoped so…for Jace's sake and for the future of the actual building.

She pulled a drawer open to check the quantity of bar towels and other necessities. This was obviously a space that hadn't been organized yet. She had a few free minutes and decided there was no time like the present. Something stuck in the jumble caught her eye. It was a magazine. Before she pitched it, she recalled the customer who left it one evening. At the time, she read the titles of a few of the articles contained inside and decided she'd take it home and read some of them. She wasn't middle-aged, by any means, but a few of them looked interesting so she might as well. Besides, it was free and the customer wasn't coming back to pick it up.

Jace was coming in after he went to the bank. He showed her the blank check the day after Emily gave it to him. He didn't know the amount to fill in until he spoke with Hubie, but he said he wanted to put it in a safe deposit box until that time. They both laughed about how they couldn't even imagine losing it and asking for a replacement.

*   *   *

Camille was taking a day off from stalking men on dating sites. It was getting wearisome. There were few men, young or old, who were truthful and it was a chore to try and sort through all the bullshit they put in their profiles. Even when a woman put in the effort to check addresses and social media sites, it was still a crap-shoot. No one governed their information so they could be Al Capone, but say they were a lonely widower or anything they wanted. She was sure it was the same on the women's sites. Granted, there were a few men she might have been interested in if she was really looking for a husband. In the last piece she sent Allie for the next issue, she told her readers the best way was still the old-fashioned way, in her opinion…meet someone in your locality and pursue a dating relationship. That was where she included the experiences with Collier and Jace. She gave no clues as to their identity so even a long lost cousin wouldn't recognize who she was referring to. She also sent an image of the blank check she wrote to Jace with her name, bank and signature blocked out.

As she was packing a sandwich and water for her little outing, Collier called. He asked if she would like to do some sight-seeing in the mountains one day.

"You must have ESP, my friend. I'm packing some lunch, as we speak. Are you free to go on this adventure today?"

"I can be if you give me thirty minutes or so. I have to finish a small project first."

When he arrived, he suggested they use his truck instead of her car. "In case, we go 'off-road' or find a canyon we want to explore," he explained. "I hope you're wearing your hiking boots."

"I am, but they're pretty new and not broken in so I think I'll take my running shoes along in case blisters begin to form."

He nodded, indicating that was a good idea. The sun was shining but the air was still chilly. He gave a running documentary as he drove, describing every bend in the road.

He wheeled his truck off the main road and onto one that seemed to be seldom used.

"Are we trespassing?"

"No," he assured her. "This is a friend's land. I come out here quite often when I need to think or regain some peace in my life. I look at the indescribable views, breathe the clean air and talk to my Maker."

After a winding drive, he found a place to park the truck. They got out of the vehicle and chose a narrow trail to begin their hike. As they climbed higher, the air became thinner and breathing was more difficult. "I think those blisters I was worried about have made an appearance," Camille said as they chose a flat rock to sit and rest for a while. She started to untie her boots when Collier knelt down in front of her.

"Let me help. As thin as the air is up here if you bend over too far you might topple over." He grinned at her and added, "I wouldn't want to have to climb down the mountain to rescue you."

From their vantage point, the view was indescribable. The mountains in the distance, the rushing stream...it all made it seem as if they were in another world.

"I never tire of these views," Collier said. "They make me fully aware of my Creator."

His statement surprised her a bit. "Do you consider yourself a religious man?"

"I guess that depends on your definition of religious. Do I believe there's a God who created me, you and all of this?" he swept his arm in an arc to indicate everything in their sight. "Yes, the answer is yes. Do I believe in organized religion? I see the necessity of it but don't necessarily want to be a part of it. Do I believe the words of the Bible? Yes." He looked at her questioningly. "How about you?"

"I don't know the answer to that question. I think I am, for the most part, a good person. I try to be unselfish, I donate to causes I like, I help old ladies across the street," she said as she smiled at him. "But, I've never had a personal relationship with God or Jesus, if that's what you mean. I've been associated with people who claim to have that but their lives don't reflect it in any visible way."

"Yeah, well that's the rebellious sinful part in all of us, I guess. You know, telling God, 'I'll believe in you but don't make me follow any of your rules' kind of thinking."

They were quiet for a while, each lost in their own thoughts.

"I know you love it here, Collier. Have you ever thought of living somewhere else?"

"Never!" was his instant answer. "I can't even imagine doing that."

Never at a loss for questions, Camille asked if he ever thought about having a family, which was one of the concerns she told her readers to delve into if they were going to pursue a relationship with a much younger man.

He shrugged. "I never thought I wanted children of my own. I've got a passel of nieces and nephews that seem like my kids without me having to support them," he added. "When I think about the shape our world is in, Camille, I don't want to bring children into it. I love kids but I'll be happy without fathering any. How about you?"

"In the beginning, I was too career-oriented. Will nor I wanted to have children, which is a good thing, as it turned out. I guess I had such a horrible relationship with my mother and I never had a father figure, so I didn't...and still don't... know what a family is supposed to look like. I don't believe I would have been good 'mother material' and obviously, at my age, it is now a moot point."

Her phone rang and she muttered, "Speaking of Mommy Dearest, it's a call from Paris. She must have changed her number; I don't recognize this one, but who else do I know in Paris, right?"

She answered with a curt, "Hello? Yes, this is Camille Desmond. Who am I speaking with?"

Her face lost all color and Collier heard her say, "When? Okay, yes, I'll make arrangements and let you know the details."

He waited for her to say something but she didn't.

"Camille? What's going on?"

"It's Barbara. She died last night."

He didn't know exactly what to do or say. He would've been more comfortable if she was crying or something, but she wasn't. He held out his arms and she went to him. He enveloped her in his embrace but didn't say anything.

"Am I supposed to be crying and carrying on now like a normal daughter?" she asked.

"I don't think there's a correct way to behave when you get news like that, but I'm here no matter what you need to do."

They sat like that for a long time until she pulled away and began to talk.

"You know, I never really had a mother. I've asked myself many times why she was so detached from me. Did she hate my father and perhaps I reminded her of him? Or did her pregnancy totally screw up some plans she had for her life? I remember asking her those questions once but she said I was being disrespectful to even ask, so I never pursued the thought again. She took good care of me...the best clothes, boarding schools, a car when I was sixteen, trips, college education...all of it. But I don't recall one hug or goodnight kiss or ever hearing her say she loved me. She didn't expect gratefulness...but obedience was high on her list. When I fought her about taking ownership of the magazine, she cut all communications with me. I did ask for her help or insight when I was being threatened with a hostile takeover. I figured she knew the magazine industry better than anyone else I knew, but she wouldn't even return my calls."

After a long pause, she added, "I was shocked she allowed me to use her house here in Montana."

Finally, she said, quietly, "I'm sad that I'm not feeling sad. If I loved her, there would be a glimmer of emotion, I'd think, but I feel nothing. My life will continue as it has...I never heard from her in the past and I'm certain I'm not going to hear from her now or in the future."

"Who was it that called you?"

"I don't know if he gave a name. If he did, I don't recall what it was. He told me she would be cremated and I needed to come to France to take possession of her 'remains' as he called them. Ugh. That sounds revolting."

Collier waited, sensing she had more to say.

"Apparently, she left detailed instructions as to the dispersal of her belongings and her home. If I know Barbara at all, there's a will somewhere and no, I do not expect to be included in it. She probably left her wealth to the local cat shelter or something like that. He did mention a letter, addressed to me. That would be her one last chance to tell me how disappointing I was to her...spoken from the grave, so to speak."

"What will you do with her ashes, Camille?"

"I don't know but I can tell you they won't sit on my mantel or anywhere in my home. That would be a constant reminder of our fractured relationship. She probably specified where she wants to be...you know, control things to the end...but if she didn't...maybe in Missouri would be good. That's where she grew up."

Quietly, barely above a whisper, Collier told her, "I'll go with you. I don't want you to go to Paris alone."

She turned to him and kissed him. The kiss was returned in a tender, passionate way.

"That isn't necessary. I've traveled by myself for many years."

"I realize that, but you've not traveled on a journey like this one. Even with the worst relationship, you can't deny she was your mother and some part of you wishes it could have been different."

Chapter 30

WHEN CAMILLE RETURNED home, she collapsed on the couch. The day had been wonderful, even after the phone call. She would wait for the gentleman who called her to call back with more information. If she wasn't needed to sort through Barbara's things, perhaps the ashes could be mailed to her. Surely mortuaries had contingency plans for circumstances like this. Not every relative would have the means to jump on a plane and fly to another country to retrieve ashes.

While she was in the midst of contemplating that problem, her phone rang again.

Maybe this was the man she spoke to earlier but when she found her phone, she saw it was Allie.

"Hey, Allie, how's everything going? Is the new issue ready to hit the streets?"

"Yes, it's already available on Amazon and will be in the stores tomorrow. That's why I'm calling you, Camille." Allie's voice sounded like she was almost in tears. That was never a good sign, as Allie was the most unflappable employee on her staff.

"Calm down, Allie. It can't be that bad. What happened? Did someone goof and put my picture back on the inside cover?" she laughed.

When there was an ominous silence on her phone, she sat up and said, "Allie! That simply is not acceptable. That cannot have happened...but it did, didn't it?"

"Oh, Camille, I'm so sorry. You can fire me if you want. It's my fault. I thought I checked everything but I handed that one responsibility to Dory and she missed that detail. I guess she was so used to seeing your photo in that spot for all these years, it seemed normal to her."

'Right. I remember how upset Dory was at the staff meeting. She didn't make a mistake…this was exactly what she wanted to happen. I should have followed my gut instinct and fired her back then.'

"Okay, okay, Allie…I'm not going to fire you, but I need to think. Maybe there's a chance we can pull it before distribution."

"We already tried, Camille. It's too late. Maybe no one in Montana will see it. After all, our distribution channels don't go west of the Mississippi."

Camille sighed and had the thought go through her head, *'You're a lot more upset about this call than you were about the previous one. What does that say about you, Camille?'*

"Well, there doesn't seem to be anything we can do at this point so we'll just have to see what happens and deal with the fallout, if there is any."

* * *

Maggie had been told to take a few days off before the band members arrived. Hopefully, things would be so busy on the weekend, she'd have to work all hours and shifts. She smiled to herself as she sat down with a cup of freshly-brewed peppermint tea, put her feet on the foot stool and opened the magazine that had been left at *The Branding Iron*. She flipped through a few recipe pages and some information on how to handle your next hospital stay. She didn't really care as she didn't foresee cooking or going to the hospital. The one she was looking for supposedly gave advice and real-life scenarios of dating sites; especially if you were an older woman seeking a younger man. Maybe she could glean some advice for Jace and his experiences on the dating site. Ah, there it was. There were several pages of anecdotes and advice. She laughed and commiserated with the author as she wrote frankly about everything. When she finished, she checked the author's name...Emily Hasbro...was that for real? How many women are named Emily Hasbro? Maybe it was a fluke, after all. That's not such an unusual name. She did want to read the next installment of this series of articles, though. The information was good as well as entertaining and useful.

Maggie went to her Amazon account and ordered the next issue. It would be in her mailbox in a few days. She was anxious to show it to Jace and give him some pointers on dating an older woman although his dating might be put on the back burner for the next two weekends.

*   *   *

Jace made sure he was available when the band members arrived. The table of regulars hung around longer than usual, just so they could meet everyone. After all, as Ken reminded them... this was his idea.

The atmosphere resembled a national holiday when the three vans pulled up outside *The Branding Iron.* Two of the vans were used to haul the equipment and the third one carried the rest of the band members and everyone's luggage. When their gigs were closer to home, they drove their own vehicles but due to the long distance this trip, they used the third van. There were introductions and handshakes all around. Of course, no one would remember names anyway...at least, not today. Introductions were first names, only.

Hubie introduced the members of the band: Seve was the drummer, Tim was introduced as the 'multi-instrumentalist,' Travis was the fiddle player and Missy, the only female in the group, played bass guitar and was the vocalist, and the person responsible for making sure everyone could hear the group, was Rod, the soundman.

Jace introduced the men at the regulars table, telling everyone they were permanent fixtures at the bar. He told them Maggie would take care of their drink requests since she was not only beautiful but the best bartender in the state of Montana. They applauded that statement while Maggie shook her head and grinned.

Mitch directed the two equipment vans to the spaces reserved for them behind the bar. It would be convenient to bring the equipment in the back doors. Ken, Ralph and the rest of the 'guys' were more than willing to help with the rearranging of tables and chairs so the band would have sufficient room and be visible to everyone.

"Don't forget to leave enough room for dancing," Maggie told them. "I might want to do a little line dancing."

They wouldn't play until tomorrow evening but perhaps tonight's customers would catch the excitement and come back tomorrow evening…with their friends.

When he could speak to Hubie privately, Jace asked about the band's fee. He wanted to get the check cashed and take care of the money concerns immediately.

Hubie frowned a bit and looked perplexed. "What are you talking about, Jace? You don't owe us anything. Our fees for both weekends and lodging, meals, everything, have been paid up front. We're good. No worries there."

"What are *you* talking about? Who paid you?"

Hubie laughed. "I'm not supposed to tell you his name but do you know a tall cowboy from Texas?"

Cal Frasier paid you?"

"He mentioned something about paying a debt of gratitude for their grandson or something like that."

Jace mumbled a few incoherent words and Hubie slapped him on the shoulder. "Enjoy the perks of the friendship, Jace," he said as he turned back to the group of people gathered around the members of the band. Everyone wanted to get their two cents worth in, forgetting they were going to be around for an entire week.

*   *   *

Jace went to his office and sat down. He was still in shock over the fact all fees had been paid. He could return Emily's check. He hadn't been feeling so good about taking it anyway. The word 'gigolo' had crossed his brain several times since she gave it to him. He did enjoy her company but didn't want to be paid for spending time with her. If that's what dating an older woman meant, he wanted no part of it. In fact, since he attended church with Dani and went to her house for dinner, he had been doing a lot of thinking about a lot of things. He was beginning to think the whole online dating thing was not for him...regardless of the age of the woman. He wanted the old-fashioned kind of dating...ask a girl out and see if you like each other, have anything in common...then if it goes well, ask her out again. He sighed. Apparently, that made him a Neanderthal in his thinking. Finding someone on the internet seemed to be the 'norm.'

CHAPTER 31

WILL WAS ENJOYING breakfast with Lorna while they discussed their upcoming business trip to New York. "I'm looking forward to spending time in The Big Apple with you, Will. I know we're required to attend the seminars during the day but the fun begins in the evening, anyway."

She was flipping through messages or emails or something on her phone when she absently asked, "Didn't you say you had a layover or changed flights or something in Bozeman, Montana on your way to California?"

He nodded. "Yes, I did. I was naively thinking I could find Camille but once I saw the size of the town, I realized how foolish that was. I had a drink at some bar named *The Branding Iron* and went back to the hotel until I could fly out in the morning. Why?"

"You remember the name of the bar?" she asked incredulously.

He grinned. "Yes, I do. I flirted a bit with the bartender…a gorgeous redhead."

Lorna didn't find that too humorous. "Ah, yes, the famous Maggie. I didn't like her and it was evident she couldn't stand me. I was going to seduce her precious Jace and although she tried, she never could get him into bed."

"When were you in Montana? A little out of your usual territory, isn't it? Out of your comfort zone?"

"The group I was working with was awarded a trip to Bozeman to experience a 'Week in the Wilderness.' Like anyone in their right mind would want to spend a week with smelly horses, campfires, insects and very few amenities of the modern world."

Will nearly choked on his food, laughing at the visions he was having of Lorna in the wilderness. "I must say, I find that quite amusing. I only wish I'd been there to observe you on the back of a horse."

"Drop dead, Will! The only decent part of the entire experience was meeting Jace. He was our guide and the owner of the *Wilderness Trips Company*. He also owned *The Branding Iron*, a bar."

"So tell me, was he good looking or rich or possibly both? That seems to be what attracts you, Lorna. Since I'm not rich, you must like me for my outstanding physique and my ruggedly handsome face."

She smiled a slow smile. "He was very handsome and I believed he was wealthy. I mean he owned two businesses for heaven's sake. Unfortunately, I found out he wasn't. In fact his bar was in financial trouble. That's when I left and went back to California."

"Of course, you did. I wouldn't expect you to stick by someone and see them through a rough time." He was joking with her but he knew his words were true.

"You are absolutely correct, my friend. I'm a firm believer in self-preservation, at all costs. I have no sympathy or empathy for people who find themselves in financial straits. It's always due to their own stupidity. Jace has obviously changed something though or inherited a windfall."

"What makes you think that?" Will asked as he proceeded to drain his coffee cup.

"I must have signed up for emails from the local newspaper when I was there and I've never taken the time to unsubscribe. I saw a half-page ad about some band playing at the bar the next two weekends. They're not local, either and they just played in Seattle at a music festival. The bar must be doing well to afford that kind of entertainment."

Will couldn't quite decide how he felt about Lorna. She was a manipulative, money-grubbing shrew, for sure. She was also intelligent, fun, sexy and a key component in helping him secure the job he wanted. *'That makes you two of a kind, Will. You probably deserve each other.'*

"We have time, Will. Let's stop in Bozeman long enough to say hello. If nothing else, it will totally tick Maggie off if I show up and who knows, if your precious Camille really is there, she might come to the bar to hear the band. Maybe we'll both get lucky." She laughed at the double meaning in that statement.

* * *

Collier called Camille to check on her. When she didn't answer, he became concerned and drove to her house. He'd been hesitant to leave her alone last night and even offered to stay and sleep on the couch...no strings attached. He knew the news of her mother's death had to affect her on some level, even if she didn't admit it. When there was no answer at the door, he walked around to the back. He found her sitting on the deck with a cup of coffee she hadn't touched, on the table beside her. She appeared to be napping but smiled at him when she heard him approach.

"What are you doing here, Collier? After playing hooky yesterday, I thought you'd have a bazillion things to accomplish today."

"A bazillion and one, to be precise. I was worried about you Camille, plain and simple."

"I'm sorry my mental state has been pushed off onto you. I'm fine, really, I am. I was following your example. I wouldn't be able to find my way back to the spot we were enjoying yesterday, so this was the next best...feeling the sun on my face and enjoying the peacefulness of the scenery and the mountains in the distance."

"Has it helped alleviate some of your worries or concerns about how to proceed with...you know, things?"

She reached out and placed her palm on his cheek. He was the kindest man she could recall ever meeting.

"Yes, I have, Collier. I spoke to the man who called yesterday. He said he was Barbara's attorney but I suspect he was more than that."

When he raised his eyebrows a bit, she nodded and stated, "Oh yes, Barbara may have been distant to me but she liked men and was always in a relationship with someone. Weird to think of your parent in those terms, isn't it? It's true and I'd be willing to bet there would be a parade of them at her funeral - if there was going to be a funeral - and if they weren't probably all deceased." She paused for a bit, then continued. "He's going to call when everything is finalized. It will be determined then if I need to be present for the reading of the will. I don't know why I would need to be there...I know she didn't will anything to me and that is perfectly fine with me."

"Do you think you'll feel up to going to *The Branding Iron* tomorrow evening? Half the

town is talking about it and I'd love to take you. Maybe a bit of dancin' will lift your spirits."

'*You better go, Camille. After all, you're the cougar who paid for the entertainment.*'

"Yes, I'd love to go with you, Collier. I'm looking forward to it."

As she watched him walk away, she wished with all her heart she had been truthful with him from the beginning. Now there were too many secrets and deceptions on her side of their friendship.

*   *   *

"What is that heavenly smell?" Dani asked as she entered the back door. She removed her work gloves and boots and proceeded to the stove where Dean was stirring something.

"Just a little beef stew with a few secret ingredients," he explained.

She kissed his cheek and told him, "Whatever it is...I'm starving. Y'know I miss Luke being here. That kid could eat a person out of house and home but it seems lonely without him. Don't you think so, Dad?"

"Yep, I do," was his only reply to her question.

"Who's joining us for dinner?" Dani asked when she saw the table set for three and her father ladling up a third bowl of stew.

"I'm baaack," Luke shouted as he appeared from the living room.

Dani laughed and jumped up to hug him. "What happened? Wouldn't they allow you on the plane? Where are your grandparents?"

"See, it's like this...they made a decision to stay and hear the band because this will probably be their last opportunity to enjoy them for a long time. They were going to surprise you but Grammy said I had to go somewhere and make myself useful because I was driving her crazy. I think she just wanted to be alone with Grandpa for a while."

"And since I can't breathe well enough to dance and Luke's not old enough to be in a bar...we're going to keep each other company while you go and have some fun, Dani."

She shook her head. "No, I don't plan on attending that circus. Besides, I don't dance."

Raising his eyebrows, her father said, "Come on now. That's not true. I saw you dancing when there was a party at the Frasier ranch in Texas. Besides, Cal and Lucy are coming to pick you up tomorrow night. You go, young lady. That's an order...you understand?"

Chapter 32

MAGGIE GRABBED HER mail as she was leaving home and threw it on the front seat of her car. She glanced at it as she did so and noticed the magazine she ordered had arrived. She certainly didn't have time to read anything today. It would be there when she did have time. She wanted to arrive at the bar early and make sure the extra wait staff Jace hired was prepared and knew what to do and where everything was located.

'Oh please, God, let this plan work like it's supposed to. If there are no customers it will be the end of The Branding Iron and maybe the end of Jace Matthews' world, as he knows it.'

As she turned onto the street where she usually parked, she was blown away by the number of vehicles already there. The advertising must have been effective…she didn't remember this many customers this early in the afternoon for a long time.

She entered through the back door and nearly collided with Mitch. "Get ready, Maggie. We've been busy for several hours already and I think we're going to be swamped this evening. I'm sure glad you and Jace had the foresight to hire enough servers."

"Yeah, me too," she answered as she walked through the tables to the bar. This was going to be a fantastic weekend. She loved being busy and serving all types of customers, especially those of the male gender. It was fun to talk and flirt and the tips should be generous tonight.

The band was scheduled to play from 7pm to 11pm. The bar was full at 5:00. Ken asked them to pose for a picture since it was his idea to hire a band, in the first place.

As the next few hours passed, people were squeezing together at tables and there was a line outside the door waiting to get inside. Cal and Lucy and a reluctant Dani arrived much earlier, knowing it would be standing room only before the band played the first note.

Collier and Camille arrived in time to secure seats at a table with another couple. They were in a far corner but could still see the band. They introduced themselves and got comfortable. Collier fought his way to the bar to get them each a drink. Maggie smiled at him and nodded her head in the direction of their table.

"Hey Sweetie, you been seein' a lot of Emily? You know, the strangest thing...I was reading this magazine and saw..." She was interrupted by Mitch asking about a certain type of whiskey a customer wanted. When she turned back, Collier had taken their drinks and was making his way back to their table. *'I'll tell him and Emily about the other person with the same name when it's not so busy. Or maybe never. It doesn't matter at all.'*

The band opened with a favorite that got everyone in the mood for a foot-stompin' evening. Hubie then took a few minutes to explain who they were and where they were from.

"We're pretty far from home but there's a few other people here tonight that might be just as far if not further. Say hello to our friends from Magnolia, Texas: the Frasiers."

"Are y'all ready for a night of foot-stompin', boot-scootin' wild Hootenanny?"

Amidst cheers, they went into the next set without further talking.

As usual, it took some time before people were comfortable getting up to dance. When they played 'Boot-Scootin' Boogie,' Hubie called out, "Come on, Cal and Lucy. Get up here and show us how it's done."

Grabbing Cal's hand, she led him to the dance floor. "Let's go, Cowboy. We can do this, for sure."

Soon the dance floor was filled to capacity as more people joined them. When Missy slowed it down a bit by singing 'Girl Crush,' Mitch looked pleadingly at Maggie and she nodded and mouthed the word, "Go!"

He practically vaulted over the bar and hurried to Dani to ask her to dance. She hesitated for only a second, then stood and followed him to the dance floor. By now, it was so crowded, it couldn't really be called dancing. Couples were close together whether they wanted to be or not.

Jace, who had been circulating all evening, glanced in their direction, frowned, paused for a bit and continued to the next table. His look wasn't lost on Lucy.

"Our Jace is jealous of whoever is dancing with Dani. I'd say that's a good thing, wouldn't you, Honey?"

Cal shook his head and hugged her. "You're not going to give up on Jace and Dani, are you, Sweetheart?"

Hubie and Travis circulated through the crowd while having a guitar and fiddle duel. Much to the crowd's delight, they jumped up onto the bar and continued playing from there.

*   *   *

"I'm going to beg off tonight, Lorna. You go find your 'used to be broke and now may be wealthy again' cowboy.' I'm going to stay here and watch a movie," Will told Lorna when they reached their hotel room. She shrugged, dismissing his words. "Suit yourself."

She was frustrated when she arrived at *The Branding Iron*. She had to park blocks away and it wasn't easy walking that far on stilettos. When she finally made her way inside, she scanned the room until she found her target. He was standing at the bar evidently waiting to take several drinks to a table. As Maggie handed them to him, she saw Lorna and nearly dropped the bottles. Lorna made her way through the crowd, quietly came up behind Jace and wrapped her arms around his waist. "I missed you, Jace. It's good to be back."

He whirled around at the sound of her voice. His jaw dropped and his mouth opened but no sound came out. Finally, he managed to say, "Lorna...what a surprise. Excuse me, I...I...have customers waiting for their beer."

There was no mistaking the look of loathing Maggie was sending in Lorna's direction. *'If that bitch is back to break his heart again, I will be sorely tempted to quietly dispose of her.'*

Maggie wasn't the only one who witnessed the encounter. It wasn't like Lorna was hard to miss. She was the only one in the room dressed as though she was a celebrity ready to walk the red carpet. Dani saw her hug Jace and felt the knot in her stomach tighten. Lucy observed the hug, also. She encouraged Dani to move toward the bar and ask Jace to dance. "Tell him he promised you this dance. That will give him an opportunity to get away from her. I don't know who she is, but he looks like he needs rescuing." When Dani shook her head, Lucy told her, "You wouldn't hesitate to rescue a calf, Dani. Now go rescue Jace." She practically pushed her in their direction.

Reluctantly, she made her way to Jace saying she was reminding him he promised her this dance. He nodded, looking slightly confused. He quickly delivered the drinks and came back to the bar to find Lorna sizing up Dani and Maggie looking as though she was going to take care of Lorna, once and for all.

Camille glanced up and came as close to having a heart attack as she ever wanted to.

'Damn! I don't know what Lorna's doing here but it's a safe bet that Will isn't far behind.'

"Collier, I have a massive headache. Could you take me home? You can come back and enjoy the remainder of the evening."

He drained his beer and stood. Grabbing her jacket, he took her arm and told her, "Come on, Emily. Let's get you home."

*   *   *

Hubie introduced each member of his band to wild applause from the crowd. The fun continued for the entire four hours with Missy singing many of the crowd's favorites. A highlight of the night was when Travis performed his rendition of 'The Devil Went Down to Georgia.' They played 'If You're Gonna Play in Texas, Ya Gotta have a Fiddle in the Band' just for Cal and Lucy.

"We appreciate everyone coming out tonight and the giant Montana welcome we received. We'll be back tomorrow evening and next weekend, too, so tell your friends and relatives and bring 'em back with you."

The crowd cheered at that statement.

* * *

As the band members prepared to leave for their hotel, a gentleman approached Hubie.

"Can I talk to you for a minute? Buy you a drink?"

"No to the drink but yes to the talking," Hubie told him.

"I thoroughly enjoyed listening to you and your band tonight. I have a lot of friends that would've loved to be here but they have younger children and as I'm sure you know, it's not always easy to find a sitter. We have a beautiful park here in Bozeman...Bogert Park...it has a band shell for a stage and a huge covered pavilion.

Do you think there'd be a chance I could talk you into a performance on Sunday afternoon? You know, a family-friendly affair. I realize it's short notice but I've already made a call this evening to the person in charge of the Parks Department and it is available. I have the resources to pay your fee. In fact, I can write you a check right now, if you'd like."

The other members of the band were gathered around, listening to the exchange. Hubie asked for their input. "We're already here and we have an entire week to fill, so I vote yes," Tim said. The others agreed with him so it was unanimous.

Hubie shook the man's hand. "Looks like you have a deal."

CHAPTER 33

LORNA REALIZED SHE left without the key card to her room. She stopped at the front desk and asked for a replacement. Handing her the card, the desk clerk also gave her a piece of paper, saying she had a message from another guest.

Lorna, I decided it would be better for both of us if I had my own room. I'm also not going to the conference with you. If you want to come to room 141in the morning, we can talk and I'll try to explain. Will

She crumpled the note and immediately walked to Will's new room. Knocking loudly and oblivious to the time, she yelled, "Will! Open this door right now. Do you hear me?!"

The door opened, he grabbed her wrist and pulled her inside. "Do I hear you? I suspect people in the next town could hear you, Lorna. You do realize most of the guests are sleeping, right?"

"What do I care? That's their problem...not mine. Why did you get another room, Will? Jealous of me going to rekindle an old flame?"

"No, not at all. Why would I be jealous? There was never anything but a flirtatious relationship between us. I'm going to be brutally honest but I highly doubt you will understand what I'm going to say. I came to California because I wanted the job you said you could help me secure...plain and simple. Was that using our friendship? Yes, it was. I'm not proud of that fact but it's the truth. I've been observing you and your

THE COUGAR AND THE COWBOY

callousness toward others, getting ahead at all costs, your mean-spiritedness and many other non-flattering traits. Unfortunately, I also see myself becoming more and more like you and that bothers me...a lot. Tonight was the last straw. You wanted to reacquaint yourself with a man you admittedly don't care about but you're interested in his cash flow. Think about it, Lorna. What's the end result here? Marriage? Because that's the only way you'd ever get your hands on his money, if he has any. How long do you think that would last with no love involved?"

She'd been pacing but stopped in front of him. "Well, aren't you just the self-righteous hypocrite all of a sudden? Who lived with Camille because they didn't have a job? You thought I didn't know about you losing your job, didn't you? Who pretended to be interested in her assistant to get her phone number? Who was that, Will? Don't pull any 'holier-than-thou' bullshit with me."

"You're absolutely correct, Lorna. I did all those things but I'm not liking myself too much for those actions. That's not who I really am and I don't want to be that way in the future but I do thank you for being my mirror so I could see myself."

"Fine. Run back to St. Louis and Camille. I'm sure she'll be waiting for you when she's done playing her 'hide-and-seek' games. I'm going to New York after I have a little fun with Jace, if I can get him alone. Tonight he danced with some girl in boots and jeans...probably some hick from this two-bit town in this God-forsaken state. I'm betting I can make him forget her if that wretched Maggie doesn't kill me first. She's just upset because she wants to get in bed with him, too. And if your precious Camille is in this town and has met him, she's probably in line, also."

She turned and moved toward the door. "I'll do my best to see to it that you never get a job in the investment industry, Will…in any state." She left, slamming the door on her way out.

'Well played, Will, ole boy. There goes your future employment and maybe enjoyment.'

He laughed at himself and the rhyme. 'The only bright spot is your foresight in buying flight insurance when you purchased your ticket. Now you can stick around for a few days before rescheduling your return flight.'

* * *

Jace sat in his recliner still fully clothed. He didn't even make an effort to remove his boots. Jake placed his head on his knee, asking for a little attention.

"I know, Jake, I've been pretty scarce around here lately, haven't I?" He rubbed the dog's head, saying, "I'm beginning to envy you. You've got a simple life, buddy. As long as I make sure you're fed and watered, you have no worries…unlike me…who seems to continue to get myself mired in messes no matter what I do."

'You should go to bed, Jace. This has been the most exhausting, exhilarating and confusing day of your life. The rodeo was hard but women are harder.'

Although he was dead tired, sleep eluded him. He said a prayer of thanks for the successful night at The Branding Iron. It was more than he ever expected. 'This praying is becoming a habit, Jace. What changed in your life that you suddenly feel comfortable talking to God again?

He didn't know the answer but he knew a few things, even in his sleep-deprived state. He knew his heart skipped a beat when he heard Lorna's voice but it almost did cartwheels when he was holding Dani in his arms and dancing with her. He also knew the line about promising her a dance was meant only to rescue him but it felt good anyway. He also knew he hadn't made it to the bank to retrieve Emily's check. He wanted to hand it back to her in person. Even though he no longer needed it, she needed to know how much he appreciated it. He wasn't sure how he felt about seeing her there with Collier last night. He was going to talk to them but when he had a few free minutes, they were gone. It would have to wait until Monday; he knew she wasn't going anywhere.

*   *   *

"So, how was the evening, Danielle?" her father asked as she came in the door.

She smiled. "You're being nosy, Dad. What is it you really want to ask?"

"He wants to know if you danced with Jace," Luke interjected into the conversation.

Still laughing, he asked, "Can I stay here another night?"

"Sure. Your grandparents are waiting for you, so go ask. Tell them it's okay with us."

Before he returned, Dani sighed. "Yes, I did dance one dance with him but he didn't ask me...I asked him. I don't know what to think or feel, Daddy. Tonight there was another woman there and she seemed pretty familiar with Jace, too. I don't want to compete with one woman, let alone three of them."

*   *   *

Collier and Camille sat on the deck, watching the stars for a while but eventually, retreated to the warmth of the house.

Removing her denim jacket, Camille told him, "Go back, Collier. Enjoy the rest of the evening. There's no reason for you to stay here with me. I'm fine."

"I know you're fine, physically, Camille. Your sudden headache appeared when the blond, over-dressed woman showed up and hugged Jace. It's your emotional health I'm worried about."

'It's time to tell him everything, Camille. He knows you're hiding a lot of secrets and he's been more than open and honest with you. If you genuinely care about him and you know you do, tell him the truth.'

She made them both a cup of peppermint tea. "I know you're not a tea drinker, but this is soothing and you may need it soon."

"Who was Miss Fancy Pants with the pearls and high heels, Camille?"

"Her name is Lorna and she's a friend of Will's. She lives in California and works for a brokerage firm. I knew if she saw me, she'd remember me. It's hard to forget the face of the woman who found you horizontal on her living room couch. She and Will were having a 'discussion' apparently, when I walked in. I was introduced as Camille and although Will wasn't with her at the bar tonight, I didn't want her to see me. He probably wasn't far behind since I believe she promised him a job or help with finding one."

"Look, Collier, I have not been honest with you about a lot of things but I've grown to like...more than like...you and it's only fair to tell you who I am and why I came to Montana."

"You don't have to if you don't want to. I think I'm falling in love with the Camille I know, or don't know, possibly."

"Don't say that, Collier. You'll change your mind. You knew I was Barbara's daughter and my name was Camille before I even arrived. If you hadn't, you would believe I was Emily, like everyone else does."

CHAPTER 34

"I TOLD YOU I write some articles for a magazine. That's true, but I think I left out the part about how I *own* the magazine, Collier. The name is *Mavis' Mag* and the offices are in St. Louis, Missouri. If some of this information is redundant, bear with me. Sadly, when a person doesn't tell the truth about things, they forget what they've said and what was left unsaid."

"The sales have been dropping over the past year...not free-falling but slowly and steadily declining. The staff and I brainstormed for several months; throwing out ideas, rejecting them, then revisiting the same ideas but with a twist of some kind."

She paused for a minute. "Did I mention the audience for the magazine is middle-aged women...anywhere from age forty to ninety or older? So, my staff and I were exhausting our brains trying to come up with something interesting and fresh. We settled on the subject of online dating but with a twist. There would be a series of articles written 'from the field' so to speak. Someone would actually become involved in online dating, write of the experiences, good and bad and give the readers tips on how to do it safely and correctly, if there is such a thing. I was the only one on the staff of the correct age, so here I am...Emily Hasbro, online dating expert."

"So you're telling me you had a date with all the men whose names I saw on your desk?"

"No, not a date with all of them. But I did interact with all of them, either through texts, e-mails, phone conversations or yes, in some cases, an actual date."

Collier was silent. Camille didn't know if he was thinking or if he was angry or disappointed or all of the above.

"Say something, Collier…anything would be okay at this point. I didn't sleep with any of them, if that counts as a plus in my favor."

"I don't really know what to say, Camille. I mean, that was a long list of names. I don't consider myself a jealous person but I cared for you and it seems to me, I was just another one of those names. The only difference was I knew your real name. Does Jace know any of this?"

She shook her head. "No and he doesn't need to. He believes my name is Emily Hasbro and I prefer we leave it at that. In a few more months, I'll go back to St. Louis and be Camille Desmond again and everything will be back to normal…for me and for you. I'm sorry if I hurt you. I never intended to fall for you or anyone else. It just happened."

Collier stood and picked up his hat. "I need some time to think through everything you told me tonight, Camille. I'll come by in the morning and we can talk some more." He gave her a kiss on the cheek and walked out the door.

"Bye, Cowboy," she said softly as he left. Wiping a tear from her cheek, she grabbed her phone and dialed a number.

"Yes, I need to schedule an early morning flight. Tomorrow. Yes, I realize it's short notice and will be expensive…I don't care."

*   *   *

The Branding Iron saw an even bigger crowd on Saturday evening than had attended Friday night. There was a line out the door and spilling onto the sidewalk with standing room only inside. Many of the people there were the same faces as last night but there were plenty of new ones, too.

Ken grabbed Jace's arm as he walked by his table and asked, "So tell me, buddy, how are you gonna top this? Got anything in mind for future weekends when Hubie and the band are back in Indiana?"

Jace shook his head. "Not anything firmed up yet but one of the customers last night told me about a band he and his friends like. They play mostly in Billings but he thought they could be persuaded to come to Bozeman."

As he walked away, Jace had what he thought was a brilliant idea...he'd put Ken and his personable ways, in charge of soliciting entertainment. He would offer to pay him of course for his time and trouble but it might serve two purposes: it would give Ken something to do besides sit at the bar and he wouldn't have to do it himself. Somehow, soliciting performers wasn't high on the top of his 'want to do' list at the moment.

As the night wore on, he saw Collier come in for a few minutes, look around the room and start to leave again. Jace caught up with him. "Aren't you staying tonight? I'll knock someone off a bar stool so you can sit down," Jace told him, laughing.

Collier shook his head. "Not tonight."

"What's wrong? And where's Emily?"

"That's what's wrong, Jace. She's gone. Disappeared. I showed up at her house this morning to tell her I was sorry about last night and the house is empty. She only brought two bags when she came and they're both gone."

Jace was frowning... "I don't understand. Where would she go? And why would she go?"

Collier shrugged. "She told me some things last night after I took her home. I didn't respond in the best way, for sure. But I was going to tell her this morning that I was sorry and I loved her, even if we haven't known each other long. As for where she went...I would assume she went back to Missouri.

She's not planning on coming back, though. The only things she bought after she got here were jeans and cowboy boots. She left those at the house with a note asking me to give them to someone."

Jace put his hand on Collier's shoulder. "I'm sorry, friend. I didn't know you felt that strongly about Emily but obviously, you do. In time, you might decide it's for the best." He looked in the direction of Lorna and said, "She left me high and dry once upon a time too, but as I look back on it, I'm glad she did."

Collier nodded and left. He would never believe it was for the best. That woman had crawled under his skin and he wouldn't forget her soon.

*   *   *

Missy's rendition of 'My Church' and 'Earl Had to Die' and Travis and Hubie's duo performances brought the people to their feet. The crowd loved every minute of it.

They never took a break, but Hubie did take the time to announce the next day's scheduled 'family friendly' concert in the park. He introduced the gentleman who hired the band to add Sunday to their schedule and handed him the microphone.

"Okay, my friends. The concert is at 1pm at Bogert Park. Bring the kids, bring your picnic lunches...heck, bring the dogs...on a leash, of course." Everyone laughed as he then continued, "Let's show these great people how we appreciate them with a Montana Sunday, okay?"

*   *   *

Jace knew he couldn't put if off any longer. He asked Lorna to come with him to his office as that was the only space available to have a conversation. Maggie saw them going that way and frowned. As soon as he closed the door, Lorna immediately put her arms around his neck and kissed him with every ounce of passion she could muster.

He was taken by surprise but recovered quickly. He removed her arms and placed them by her side. "Listen to me, Lorna. I have no idea what brought you back to Montana but you and I both know it wasn't just to kiss me, okay? What we had when you were here for your week in the wilderness experience was just that…a wilderness experience. We didn't know each other and still don't, really."

"I'd like to remedy that situation, Jace. We could get to know each other much better if you'd give it a chance."

She brought her arms up again but he caught them this time. "No, that isn't going to happen, Lorna. What we had was a small infatuation…nothing more. And, the minute you found out I had no money, you disappeared. I suspect you thought when you saw the crowds out there, that *The Branding Iron* was more than successful now but that isn't true. In fact, a friend loaned me the money to bring that band here to try and raise awareness of this place."

She pursed her lips into a pouty little girl face and whined, "But Jace, I do care about you."

The door opened and Maggie stuck her head in. "Sorry, Boss but there's a situation out here I think you need to take care of."

Jace left immediately, envisioning a bar fight. Maggie stepped into the room and closed the door behind her when he left, blocking Lorna's exit. She put her hands on her hips and looked at Lorna. "Now listen and listen good, you money-grubbing bitch. You are never going to get your hooks into that man, do you understand me? He's a good man and deserves a good woman and that isn't you. Now I want you out of *The Branding Iron* in the next ten minutes and if you ever come back, I will kick your ass all the way back to California. Consider yourself lucky I'm only using words right now." She walked behind Lorna all the way to the front door, escorting her out into the night.

Jace couldn't find any problem to take care of but he did see Lorna storm out the door. Maggie came back to the bar and smiled at him. "It's all good, Boss. I just took the trash out."

Chapter 35

ON THE FLIGHT Camille had a thousand thoughts running through her head. It made her unbelievably sad to know she would, in all probability, never see Collier again. Her fake phone number and email address would be eliminated and he would not be able to reach her, even if he wanted to...which she was sure he didn't.

She would continue writing the articles using the name Emily Hasbro. She had experienced enough different kinds of scam artists, genuine people and just plain wierdos that she should be able to fictionalize most of the columns.

'Why did you ever think this would work in the first place, Camille? You've never considered yourself to be an accomplished liar so what possessed you to think you could pull this off? You should have turned around and headed right back home the minute you met Collier and realized he knew who you were. Woulda, shoulda, coulda...the story of your life.'

* * *

Dani didn't go back to the bar on Saturday evening, choosing to stay home with her dad and Luke. After the concert in the park on Sunday, the Frasier family really was leaving for Texas and she wanted to spend some time with Luke while Cal and Lucy went to enjoy the band one last time. Luke and her dad had developed a special bond during the weeks he was visiting and she knew Dean would miss him.

"We are going to the park tomorrow, right?" Luke asked. "I want to hear the band too so I know what Grandpa and Grammy are talking about all the way home," he confessed.

"Of course, we're going, aren't we, Danielle?"

She looked at her dad and made a face. "I know what you're up to, Dad and it isn't going to work, but yes, we'll pack a picnic lunch and go to Bogert Park."

Dean and Luke gave each other a conspiratorial grin. Dani didn't know for sure what that was all about but she was certain it had something to do with her and Jace.

*   *   *

When Cal and Lucy were dancing, she whispered in his ear, "That woman I said I didn't know but was putting the moves on Jace...she left in a huff. That's one down."

"What in the world are you talkin' about, Lucy?"

"Oh Honey, you're so unobservant sometimes. The way I have it figured, there's three or four women wanting to get closer to Jace. The blond who just left...I think we can consider her gone. The one who was with the man named Collier, last night...mmm, I think she kind of liked him too. Then there's the bartender, Maggie. I like her a lot and she confided in me last night that she's been after Jace for a few years but strictly on a 'go to bed' mission. Then there's Dani who won't admit how much she cares for him. I'm praying for Dani. How about you?"

"I'm still trying to figure out how you surmised all that just by watching people."

*   *   *

Will had a flight back to St. Louis in the morning so he decided to spend some time at the bar he went to the first time he was in town. He was amazed at the crowd. The last time he was there, it was fairly empty. He found a seat at the bar when someone moved.

The same bartender waited on him. "Hey, good to see you're back," she said with a beautiful smile.

"I'm flattered you remembered me," he told her.

"I never forget a handsome face and a good tipper," she joked.

"And I never forget a beautiful redhead, either. It's Maggie, right?"

"You, sir, have a fantastic memory. What can I get for you tonight?"

Will ordered and watched her as she moved around the busy bar area. She was good at her job for sure and easy on the eyes, too.

When she came back to see if he needed a refill, she told him, "Y'know, you left a magazine here. I kept it for a while but then I took it home and read it. It's still at my place so I'm afraid I can't give it back."

He shrugged. "No problem. I know the editor and owner and occasionally I buy a copy just to see what's being published for women who are close to my age."

Maggie squinted at him. "And that would be about...hmm...forty or forty-five?"

"You flatter me, Miss Maggie. There would have been fifty candles on my last birthday cake, if I'd had one. A cake, that is." She chuckled at that.

"You know, I was thinking my friend might be here in Bozeman. You don't recall hearing the name, Camille Desmond, do you?" He glanced around the crowded room.

Shaking her head, Maggie said, "No, I haven't and I do know a lot of people in Bozeman and surrounding areas. It's one of the perks or drawbacks of my job, depending on how you look at it."

Mitch hurried around the end of the bar, almost colliding with Maggie.

"What are you doing, Mitch? Somebody chasin' you?"

"Oh my gosh, Maggie. Larry was working at the grill when he suddenly said he felt dizzy. If I hadn't caught him, he would've ended up on the floor. His cousin was here tonight and volunteered to take him to the after-hours clinic but we're gonna have to shut the kitchen down and there's still a bunch of orders hangin up waitin' to be made."

"Well, crap!" was Maggie's undignified reply. "I am not a grill cook by any stretch of the imagination. Go ask Jace if he can fill in. Hurry. We don't want to lose the new customers we just found."

Will watched all the commotion and debated if he wanted to get involved. *'You said you wanted to return to being a good person.'*

"Hey Maggie, if your boss won't mind a stranger in the kitchen, I could help you out. I was a grill cook in high school and college. I wield a mean spatula. By the way, my name is Will."

Before he was done talking, Maggie had him behind the bar and was tying an apron around his waist.

"At this point, I don't care if your name is Attila the Hun...you're hired."

When the kitchen closed, Jace thanked Will. "You saved our butts tonight. How can I ever thank you?" He pressed some bills into Will's hand, which he promptly returned.

"I can't take your money. I had a blast. I haven't had to physically work that hard or that fast for many years. It was great fun. I should be paying you."

"If you ever come back through Bozeman, make sure you stop in to see us."

Will smiled and handed Maggie his card. Then he looked at Jace. "If you give this beautiful creature a vacation, send her to St. Louis, okay?"

He grabbed his jacket from the bar stool where he left it and slung it over his shoulder. Then he quickly kissed Maggie and walked out the door.

*   *   *

When the evening drew to a close, Cal invited Jace to attend church with them again in the morning. Glancing at his watch, he said, "We can attend late service and then head straight to the park. What do you say? Luke will be looking for you and I think you enjoyed it last week."

Jace didn't want to go. He was whipped after three days of non-stop activity, if you counted the day the band arrived and set up. The thought of seeing Dani again went through his mind and he agreed. "You twisted my arm, Cal. I'll be there."

*   *   *

Maggie slept in on Sunday morning. She might wander over to the park in the afternoon just to take pictures of the crowd she was certain would show up but this time, she could enjoy the music without having to take orders for drinks. She made herself a cup of tea and lounged around in her pajamas, enjoying the solitude. It took half the night and into the morning before her ears stopped ringing from the crowd last night and before she stopped thinking about that last-minute kiss. She took her tea and a piece of toast to the porch. As she glanced at the pile of mail she had tossed onto a chair for the last two days, she remembered the magazine she ordered from Amazon.

'You might as well read the rest of the information about being a cougar and enjoying the company of a younger man, Maggie. You're not getting any younger and Jace isn't getting any more willing.'

She turned to the inside cover and table of contents. While scanning the names of articles to find the page number for the dating one, she noticed this issue had the picture of the editor-in-chief along with her name. She looked at it and then looked a second time...unless Emily Hasbro had an identical twin, that was her in the picture but the name was Camille Desmond. *'What the hell?!'*

CHAPTER 36

SUNDAY MORNING DAWNED bright and sunny; it was going to be a good day for a concert and picnic in the park. Jace looked at his alarm clock and in his head, he listed all the reasons he did not want to get up and go to church. His leg and hip were causing him pain with every move he made. The extra activities of the past few days and the lack of rest were doing a number on the damaged nerves. He rolled over onto his back and stared at the ceiling. There were so many thoughts going through his sleepy brain this morning.

'I have to retrieve Emily's check from the bank but if she's gone, I can't return it...guess I'll just destroy it. I feel bad for Collier. I wasn't aware he had been that interested in Emily. I would love to have been a fly on the wall when Maggie was talking to Lorna...whew. The weekend was phenomenal...better than I could have hoped for in my wildest dreams. Receipts from the first night were better than a month's receipts formerly and there were even more people last night. Thank you, Lord and thank you, Cal and Lucy. I guess if I want to say goodbye to them and Luke, I'd better get my butt out of bed and take a shower.'

Jace arrived at church a few minutes late and slid in the pew next to Dani's father. It was the only seat left but he wished it had been next to Dani instead. The sermon was about acceptance...acceptance of our fears, our hurts and our circumstances, whatever they might be. Jace realized he had never accepted his injuries although they were the consequences of a lifestyle and occupation that he chose, knowing full well what the dangers were. The longer he listened, the more things he knew he had not totally accepted: his mother leaving, his dad remarrying, his loneliness and the fact he would, in all likelihood, never have the family he craved. It was time to accept all of those things and his responsibility for his life…and God's forgiveness and acceptance of him…just as he was.

*   *   *

The parking spaces were becoming scarce by the time their group arrived at the park. Chairs, blankets and food baskets were everywhere, it seemed…on the grass and in the pavilion. If the event was judged by the number of children running around, it was already a success.

*   *   *

Luke was enjoying all the food Dani and Dean packed plus what Cal and Lucy brought, while he waited patiently for the band to begin playing. A small group of children ran in front of them. When one tripped, Jace stood him back on his feet and brushed the grass off his knees.

Luke told him, "You know what I think, Jace? I think you ought to marry Dani and have lots of kids of your own, like my mom and dad do. You'd make a great dad."

Jace and Dani glanced at each other and then everyone burst out laughing.

"Thank you for your insight on that, Luke but I suppose we should have at least one date before I ask her to marry me, don'tcha think?"

"Yeah, that'd be good, I guess. So when are you going to ask her for a date?"

Jace looked at Dani again and said, "Do you think you'd like to have dinner tomorrow night?"

She smiled and observed, "Sure. No pressure or anything."

Blakely was striding toward Jace and seemed bent on saying something before the concert started.

He held out his hand and Jace took it. "I want to congratulate you. You pulled it off when I didn't think you had a prayer of saving *The Branding Iron*. I don't know how and I don't care but I want you to know I'm a businessman. I didn't want your bar just to tear it down but I saw an opportunity and I was going to take it. Since it seems it's now on the road to being successful, I'll leave you alone. But don't let it slip…I'll still be in the wings, watching."

Jace smiled, "Maybe it was a prayer that saved it, Blakeley, or perhaps," as he looked in the direction of his friends, "many prayers."

* * *

Maggie showered and got dressed. She had to show Jace and Collier the magazine and the picture of Camille or Emily or whoever she was. She was a fraud, for sure. After she read the article, she recognized two of the men on her 'cougar' list were Jace and Collier. They weren't named, of course, but she knew it was them and the dating experiences matched up. Although the one she perceived to be Jace described a pretty steamy encounter and that didn't seem quite right to her. She wrote their names in permanent marker on the specific parts of each column so they could find them easily. Otherwise, she knew neither one of them would read far enough to agree with her.

By the time she arrived at the park, she had cooled down a bit but went in search of Jace, anyway. When she found him and the group, she made the decision to confront him with the magazine article at another time. This wasn't the place. She said hello and moved on to join some other friends of hers.

*   *   *

Camille lay on her bed in a hotel room in Paris. Since it was Sunday, she couldn't meet with the attorneys until tomorrow. She knew she couldn't stay inside all day. After showering and dressing in some casual clothes, she went for a walk. Wandering aimlessly, with no destination in mind, she came to a church and decided to step inside. She slid into a pew in the very back and closed her eyes to enjoy the strains of an organ. While she didn't understand the words, the music afforded her a sense of peace and calm that she didn't recall feeling in her entire life. *Would her life be better if she wasn't consumed with success and also dislike for her mother? Probably.* She felt comfortable and at peace when she was with Collier. He had a stabilizing effect on her and she felt that she loved him but it was too late for that now.

*   *   *

As people prepared to leave the park after the concert, there were hugs all around as the Frasier family was catching an early flight back to Texas in the morning. Jace thanked them again for their friendship and their generosity. Then he excused himself and spoke to the band members. He offered guided trail rides during the week to any of them who would like to ride for a few hours. He suggested they might need to relieve some boredom once they rested up from their weekend.

He walked with Dani and Dean to their vehicle. Opening the door for her, he asked, "So were you serious when you said you'd have dinner with me or were you placating Luke?"

She looked him directly in the eyes and said, "I will have dinner with you, Jace."

CHAPTER 37

WHEN JACE ARRIVED at the bar on Monday morning, he was greeted by Ken, Harry and the rest of the regulars, all sitting at the same table as usual, drinking coffee and acting as if nothing changed.

"We're here early, Jace-man, because if we got it figured right, the new lunch crowd is gonna squeeze us out. And we're good with that."

Jace poured a cup of coffee and sat down with them.

"It has been a ride, hasn't it? Unbelievable. I keep pinching myself to make sure I'm not dreaming."

"Well, if you're dreaming, we're all in the same dream," Ken laughed. "But I've got a question...I asked the other night but didn't get an answer. How are we going to keep up the momentum?"

Jace pushed his hat back and smiled at him. "That's something I want to talk to you about, my friend."

Everyone at the table laughed. "Be careful. When he calls you 'my friend' in that tone of voice, you're in trouble."

Jace explained his idea of hiring Ken to be his scout for entertainment, since he knew everyone in six counties.

Ken looked serious and told him he would consider it. "It might even allow me to talk to other good lookin' women since Maggie won't give me the time of day," he declared as he winked at her.

She just shook her head. "I need to talk to you for a minute, Jace, when you're done with your conversation."

"That sounds serious. You better go."

Jace walked to the bar and looked questioningly at her. "Does this have to do with Larry and his availability to work?"

"He's fine. Had a touch of the flu, I guess but he'll be back this evening. That's not what I want to talk to you about. Come to the office with me."

"Watch out, Jace. She's still after you." That was followed by raucous laughter.

"So, what's up?"

She placed the magazine on his desk and pointed to the picture. "She look familiar to you?"

He picked it up and frowned. "Camille? But she said her name was Emily. What is this?" he asked as he looked at the front cover.

"It's a women's magazine, Jace. For middle-aged women, precisely. She not only is the senior editor, she owns the damned thing. She wasn't vacationing here...she was working. That work included dating younger men and writing about the experiences. I think this article is about you and I must confess, if it's true, I am very jealous. And...I think this one describes Collier."

* * *

Camille arrived at the offices she had been directed to on the third floor. She was ushered into a tastefully furnished suite, had a chair pulled out for her and was offered a beverage.

"Ms. Camille Desmond?" the man questioned.

She nodded and showed him her identification. She was surprised there were no other people in the room. Either Barbara didn't have anything left to bequeath to someone or they didn't care. She really didn't care either, knowing she would inherit nothing, which was fine with her. She wanted nothing but the message she received stipulated she would need to accept Barbara's ashes and they would not send them to her. So here she was.

"The first order of business is your mother's ashes." He indicated a simple walnut box.

"I don't mean to be rude by interrupting but are you certain you have the correct container? Barbara would never lower her standards enough to have her remains placed in a wooden box, of all things."

"I assure you this is the correct container. We are extremely judicious in our proceedings and have worked with this reputable crematorium for many years."

Camille shrugged. She didn't understand but also didn't care.

He cleared his throat and proceeded. "Your mother specified that the box not be mailed to you but rather, that you were to come to Paris to retrieve it."

"The next order of business this morning is the will. Since you are the only individual named in the will, there should be no contesting and we can finish this in an expedient manner."

She tapped her foot incessantly while he droned on about the legality of certain things and then cleared his throat again.

"You have inherited the property in Montana, the stocks and bonds and a snow globe."

She raised her hand to stop him. "Back up just a bit...a snow globe? Did you say I inherited a snow globe?"

He looked at her over the top of his spectacles. "Yes, that's what it says. A snow globe. May I continue?"

Camille nodded and tried desperately to pay attention but her train of thought got off at the station when he said snow globe.

"All of her possessions here in Paris, including the property she owned, have been sold and the profits donated to her favorite charity, as per her instructions. I have the paperwork to verify that. And now, one last thing..." He opened a drawer, withdrew a slim mauve-colored envelope and placed it on the desk. "This is a letter for you from Barbara but you are not to read it until you're back home in Missouri. Of course, I have no control over that once you leave this office but that's what she wanted."

Camille thanked him, placed the envelope into her bag, picked up the walnut box and the box containing the snow globe and walked out the door.

'That was the most bizarre experience I've had in my entire life, I believe. Don't open the envelope until I'm home? Still controlling things, aren't you, Barbara? Even after death.'

*   *   *

She returned to her hotel, gathered her few bags and left for the airport. She'd booked a flight for St. Louis in the afternoon, knowing the meeting would most likely be brief. It was, but not for the reason she expected.

On the long trip home, she tried to imagine what the envelope contained. Probably more admonitions about how to live her life and how disappointed Barbara was with the life Camille already lived. She would honor Barbara's wishes and wait until she was sitting on her own couch in her own living room with a glass of her own wine in her hand. Perhaps a bottle, instead.

She took a cab home from the airport and was perplexed to see another cab at the curb.

She had to laugh when Will got out and rolled his bags up the front sidewalk. She startled him when she called out, "Isn't this a coincidence? Both prodigals return at exactly the same time."

CHAPTER 38

AFTER UNPACKING AND getting comfortable in her pajamas, Camille poured the glass of wine and curled up on the couch with her legs tucked under her. She was extremely tired and debating about reading the letter tonight or waiting until morning when she might be more able to function.

Will came into the room and sat down next to her.

"Tired?" he asked.

"Beyond exhaustion, Will," she admitted, laying her head on his shoulder.

"Do you want to talk about the last few months?"

"Maybe tomorrow. It would require too much energy and emotion right now. How about you?"

"I'm not sure I can even put my feelings into words. Something happened while I was gone. I believe I'm a different person in several areas of my life but I'm still assessing the situation."

She chuckled at that. "Yeah, me too. I forgot to tell you...Barbara died."

He pushed himself to a sitting position on the edge of the couch so he was looking into her face. "You *forgot* to tell me?"

"It's been something I had to come to terms with and I don't think that will fully happen until I read her last instructions to me." She held up the letter she had laying on her lap.

Will sat back and put his arms around her. "I'm sorry, Camille. I wish I could say I liked her, but that would be a lie. However, I do love you and I don't want you to hurt."

She lifted the flap on the envelope and withdrew several folded sheets of paper.

"Will you stay with me while I read this?" she asked.

"Of course...and when you get to the part about how you made a huge mistake when you married me...I'll plug my ears."

My dearest Camille,

I know you already think this letter is a fake if I started it with calling you 'my dearest' but I assure you it is real. This dying business does strange things to a person, including making me look back at my life with a totally different perspective. It's a pity we can't see things as clearly through healthy eyes as we can when they are clouded with the knowledge of our impending death. That's enough about my demise; I have many things to tell you.

You came into my life at a very inconvenient time for me. I never, in a million years, believed I could conceive...doctors told me it was impossible. To say I was not prepared to be a mother would be expressing it mildly. It didn't help to have forty-eight hours of labor. You wanted to do things your way from the very beginning, including exiting the birth canal. Your way, your timing. From birth, you fought me on everything: what to eat, what to wear, which toys to play with...and you weren't a rebellious teen at the time...you were a toddler.

Our relationship was always the 'oil and water' type. You may have believed my sending you to boarding schools, summer camp and every other type of learning experience was for your education, when in reality, it was for our preservation. I always believed the best way to be your mother was to be an absent one.

My mother, your grandmother, had amassed a small fortune publishing 'Mavis' Mag.' I reaped the benefits but hated the magazine. I hated it for two reasons: my mother was totally engrossed in the publication and had no time for me... and as I became older, it represented the world I was expected to embrace: late marriage, becoming a grandmother, employment, retiring spouses, how to dress as a middle-aged woman...all concepts I abhorred.

When you met William and immediately wanted to marry him, I fought you. I had nothing against him personally; I simply didn't think it was a good idea for you to get married and because I expressed those thoughts, you did the opposite and married him. I'm certain my meddling and interfering was responsible for your divorce but I wasn't sorry it happened.

When I refused ownership of the magazine and your grandmother offered you the opportunity, I was sure you didn't possess the experience or toughness to handle it. I was wrong. I saw you were doing an outstanding job. Mavis' Mag was gaining readership and sales despite my best efforts to derail your success.

Camille, I had many contacts in the publishing world who kept me informed about you and your life. I saw your job becoming all-consuming. You had no life, no family, no friends outside of work and no interests or hobbies. It was going to kill you and to what end? So your tombstone could say, SHE OWNED A MAGAZINE?

I initiated the hostile takeover a few years ago. I won't go into all the details but it would have succeeded if Will hadn't done a bit of insider trading which forced my contacts to back off. I had my attorney threaten you and Will with charges and collusion. I never had him actually file the charges. All of this was done without using my name so you would never know. However, I don't want you to live in fear of being prosecuted any longer so I'm telling you. I wanted desperately to save you from yourself.

Camille stopped reading and looked at Will. "I can't even think of enough expletives to say right now."

Will was laughing so hard, he nearly choked. "She was quite the manipulator. Wow. I never suspected it was her."

"How can you find any humor in this?"

"The humor is in the fact that I chased those damned legal papers you kept in your safe all the way to Montana."

"Is that why you tried calling me?"

"Yes. I wanted the combination to your safe. I needed to read those documents from the attorney to know if the statute of limitations was up before I applied at the firm in California. I finally decided to take my chances and now...with this," he pointed to the letter..."there were never any legitimate charges anyway. How many years have we waited for the shoe to drop?"

Camille shook her head. "If she was so worried about my mental state, what did she think having jail time hanging over my head was doing to it?"

She continued reading: *I know you don't need my Paris house or my furnishings, so as I'm sure the attorney told you, I've left instructions for them to be sold and the proceeds donated to charity. The only things I'm leaving for you are some stocks and bonds, the house in Montana and the snow globe and there's a reason for each one.*

You never liked what I purchased for your Christmas gift regardless of what it was. I spent a lot of money to get the right things only to fail year after year. One year, I decided I was done trying. I bought the cheap snow globe and stuffed it in a gift bag. You pretended to hate it, but I saw you turning it over again and again. I've kept it to symbolize the one and only time we agreed on something. I thought perhaps you would enjoy having it...perhaps not. It's yours now, do with it what you want.

I only spent a few weeks each year at the Montana house but I always felt peaceful and grounded when I was there. It gave me comfort and a perspective on my life I couldn't attain anywhere else.

The last time I was there, I had recently been told I didn't have too long to live. I sat on the deck and made a conscious decision to not do a damned thing about it. I chose to fill my remaining years, months, weeks or days with as many of my favorite activities as I could. I did not tell you or anyone else except your father. He was always a praying man, which I scoffed at then, but I asked him to pray for you, Camille, not for me.

I have been a cold, unemotional mother and for that, I ask your forgiveness. Please don't wait until you are dying to realize there's more to life than work and money. There's love and contentment. Go find it. (And for once in your life, don't fight me on this.)

Loving thoughts of you, Camille,

Barbara

CHAPTER 39

JACE WAS TRYING to absorb everything Maggie was saying but she was agitated enough that her words were coming at him in unintelligible half-sentences.

"Slow down, Maggie. It can't be that bad. I really don't see the harm in Emily or Camille or whatever her name is writing with a different name. Authors do it all the time."

"But...but, did you even read what she wrote about you?" She stabbed the article with her finger.

"What makes you so sure she's writing about me? I glanced at it and didn't see any names, whatsoever."

She grabbed the magazine and left the office, slamming the door. "Men...they're so damned dense sometimes!"

She threw the folded publication under the bar and continued mumbling to herself.

She fished her phone out of her pocket when it buzzed. "Hello?" she answered in an annoyed voice.

"Is this a bad time, Maggie?"

"It could be. Who is this?"

"It's Will...your fill-in grill cook. How quickly you've forgotten me. I'm hurt."

"And I'm sorry. I haven't forgotten you, Will. I've just had a conversation that didn't leave me in a very good humor. Where are you?"

"I'm in St. Louis. But I'm thinking of heading back to Bozeman for a few weeks or a month and wondered if you'd consider going out with me while I'm there."

"Yes, of course I'd love to show you around. We have enough beautiful scenery around here to last for months of sightseeing."

"That's good. I have some loose ends to tie up here before I leave. I'll let you know when I'm getting ready to head your way."

* * *

Camille came down the stairs still in her robe. "I sincerely hope you've made a pot of coffee, Will, if you're up this early."

"Yes, ma'am, I've got it all ready for you…in your favorite cup, even."

She took the proffered cup and sat on a stool at the kitchen island. As she looked at him over the rim of the cup, she asked, "What are you grinning about?"

"Truthfully, I never went to sleep last night. My mind was way too busy."

"I had trouble sleeping too but probably for different reasons."

"You tell me your reasons and I'll tell you mine," he said in a little boy voice.

"You're entirely too happy. Did you spike the coffee?"

He shook his head. "No, I didn't. I've done a lot of self-introspection and made decisions based on what I discovered."

"Can't say I was immersed in psychological introspection. I was mostly thinking about Barbara's letter."

"Yeah, that was part of my thinking, also. But I have to thank Lorna for my new-found outlook on my life."

Camille rolled her eyes and took another swallow of coffee. "Please…spare me. Lorna doesn't seem to have any positive effects on anyone she comes in contact with."

"Ahhh, but you see, when I had to spend time with her, I became aware of the fact I was slowly becoming more and more like her and I didn't like what I saw. Self-absorbed, no regard for others, hurting people, getting ahead at all costs...you know, all those sterling traits."

She nodded and refilled her cup. "Yes, I do know and you could be describing me, also. Do you have a solution to our despicable characters or should we accept our faults and revisit our relationship, since no one could possibly love either of us...except each other?"

He reached for her hand. "As inviting as that sounds, my love, I don't believe it would work any better this time around than it did the last time, even without interference from your mother. And in your heart, you believe that too. I feel as though Barbara's advice about life has lifted a big burden from my shoulders. I'm going to pursue a path in cooking, as you've advised me to do for many years. When I was in Bozeman, I filled in for a sick grill cook for an evening and remembered how much satisfaction it gave me."

"You're surely not going to be able to survive on a grill cook's wages. That can't pay more than minimum, Will."

"I know, but the adrenaline rush of having to have everything ready at the same time, make it look good and remembering all the details plus be fast at it...that was exhilarating. I think I'm going to go back and see if I can at least fill in for a few weeks at *The Branding Iron* while I decide how far I want to go with this idea."

Camille threw her head back and laughed. "I don't suppose that delicious redhead named Maggie has anything to do with this momentous decision, does she?"

Grinning, Will answered, "That might have swayed me a bit." More seriously, he added, "Why don't you come with me, Camille? You have a home there now and no one at the magazine knows you're back. They will never know you even came back to Missouri."

She looked thoughtful. "I suppose I have to return at some time to file papers on the property, transferring it to my name, although Barbara, in her efficiency and control mode, probably already took care of that."

"I never asked how your secret project went or exactly what it was or if it's finished or what?"

She sighed. "It went famously well. I was writing articles from the field of actual online dating experiences. All kinds but with emphasis on the 'cougar' type: you know, older woman, younger man. It was actually a lot of fun and very enlightening. I had no idea the expertise it requires to separate the authentic people from the fake. It's amazing how many scammers are out there, waiting to prey on unsuspecting women. There's always the good news, I guess, that a woman could find someone they were attracted to and fall hard for him."

"Is that what happened to you, Camille?" Will asked softly.

She waved her hand to indicate he was way off base. "No…well maybe. But the age difference is too great. It would never work."

"Wait a minute. Isn't that what you were writing about? I read some of your articles on the plane…yes, I bought a copy of Mavis' Mag…and you seemed to be encouraging women to fall in love with the right guy, no matter what the age difference. Obviously, you aren't taking your own advice."

"I don't know, Will. I think it may have worked before he discovered I'd been lying all along. That's not a good foundation for a relationship."

"True. But do you want to accompany me to Bozeman or not? This is the perfect time since you aren't expected or needed at the magazine."

"And you'd have a place to live, right?"

"You are so suspicious but yes, perhaps I could live in your house until I got a paycheck of some kind. I can pay rent and this time, I really will. Despite what I told you about living here, I'm not destitute."

"All right. Pick the day and we'll leave on our adventurous road trip. I need to contact a few people first and you said you had some loose ends to tie up?"

He nodded. "I do."

Camille left the kitchen and Will dialed a number. When he heard her answer, he spoke quickly before she could hang up. "Allie, please don't hang up on me. I don't want anything from you but forgiveness. Allow me to take you to lunch and I promise you won't recognize the penitent me. I won't even mention Camille's name."

CHAPTER 40

WILL SAUNTERED INTO *The Branding Iron* trying to keep a straight face but it wasn't possible. Once he saw the look on Maggie's face, he started laughing.

"Here I am, ma'am. Your new grill cook reporting for duty."

"You're kidding me, right?" was her reply.

"Nope. I contacted Jace when you and I spoke on the phone and during that conversation, you said he was putting an ad in the paper. He told me to come on out and we'd give it a try."

"I can't believe this. Who, in their right mind, chooses sweating in a bar kitchen over working in a prestigious investment firm?"

He cleared his throat. "That would be me, I guess, but no claims about being in my right mind."

"Where are you staying and seriously, Will, how long do you plan to do this? As much as I love the idea of working with you, I don't want Larry to have to train you and then train someone new in a week or two when you've had your little fling."

"I can't guarantee staying long-term, Maggie, but it will be longer than a few weeks...promise. I'm looking into an apprenticeship at a restaurant in Billings, but this can't hurt my resume. A well-rounded chef should have experience in all types of establishments. I made Jace aware of my plans when we spoke. There are no more secrets in my life. It's too difficult to keep track of things we say when only half of it is true."

She nodded in agreement, then grabbed a clean apron and helped him put it on. "Where did you say you were staying? I'm only asking so I can tell you how long it might take you to get to work at certain times of the day."

"I'm staying at the house on Flagler Rd. Yes, the same one...Camille's house."

Maggie stopped tying the strings of the apron and just stood there, looking at him.

He put a hand on each of her arms and sat her down. There were only a few customers so he pulled a chair up beside her. "Listen to me, Maggie. I told you I would tell the truth, no matter what. Many, and I mean many, years ago, Camille and I were married...we were still in college. Due to many factors, it ended in divorce. However, we have been close friends ever since...sometimes hating each other...but always being there for each other. I guarantee you we are not 'friends with benefits'. We have lived together, off and on but we have not slept together since the divorce. Please believe me. It's important to me that you believe me."

"I don't know what to say. I'm not fond of your ex-wife at the moment. I wouldn't believe anything she had to say. She deceived all of us and in doing so, she probably messed up some people's lives. People I care about. The lies she wrote in her little magazine were just that...lies."

"Yes, I'm sure they were but in the publishing world, it isn't lying. It's called embellishing the truth to connect with the readers. She didn't mention any names or locations, did she?"

"No. But I know the one encounter she described was with Jace. I could tell."

"So, tell me, are you upset because you think she lied about Jace or because it might have actually been Jace?"

"I don't know, Will. Now that you've asked me, I'd have to say it made me very jealous." She laughed a bit and confessed, "I've been trying to get that man undressed and in bed for so long, I couldn't stand to read about some other woman unbuttoning his shirt."

"I understand. Maybe you need to focus your fantasies on someone else."

She nodded and smiled a little, "Perhaps you're right."

Jace came out of his office, crossed the floor to where they were sitting and shook hands with Will.

"I see you made it back to Bozeman. Like everyone else, once you're here, you never want to leave for long. Did you have a good trip?"

"Yes. It doesn't take long when you have two drivers."

Jace gave him a questioning look. "Did Emily come back with you?"

Will nodded and Maggie rolled her eyes as she corrected him, "Her name's Camille,

Jace. You can't call her Emily any longer."

"Great. I have some unfinished business with her." He went behind the bar and grabbed the magazine to take with him. Then he changed his mind, threw it on the bar and went out through the office and the back door, instead, saying, "I don't need to take that with me."

* * *

While Mitch was cleaning up and Larry was giving Will instructions, Dani came in the door. Mitch's face lit up like a candle.

"Hi Dani. What brings you in here?"

"I dropped Dad at the doctor's office but they're running way behind today. I didn't want to sit there but don't want to

spend the time and gas to go home either, so I thought I'd
come here and drink lemonade for a while."

"That's great," Mitch told her as he put a glass of ice cold
lemonade in front of her.

He went back to cleaning while she sipped the cold drink.
When she spied a rolled up magazine on the bar, she opened it
to read while she waited. When checking the cover, she saw it
was for middle-aged women but since it was the only thing
available to pass the time she decided it would be better than
nothing. She scanned the recipes and vacation tips. When she
reached the feature article, she saw someone had written JACE
on the one column with a Sharpie. There was another name
scribbled on the next page...COLLIER. She began reading the
words but her face contorted before she got to the end.

"I have to go, Mitch. Thanks for the lemonade. Dad's
waiting for me." She slid off the stool and practically ran out
the door.

When Maggie returned, she asked, "Did I see Dani in here?"

"Yes, for a little bit," Mitch answered with a bewildered
look.

"Why did she leave without saying hello?"

"Don't ask me. One minute she was reading a magazine
and the next minute, she was gone."

Maggie realized what Dani had been reading which
wouldn't have been a problem if she hadn't written Jace and
Collier's names on the pieces she was convinced were about
them. She never meant for anyone but the two men to see it.

* * *

Dean got into the truck and was talking to Dani but she wasn't
replying.

"What's the matter...cat got your tongue?"

She shook her head but didn't say anything. That's when he noticed the few tears on her face.

"Awww, Honey. What's the matter? Please don't cry. I never could stand to see my girl cry. Tell me what happened."

"It's complicated and I don't even know how to explain it, Dad, because I don't understand what's going on. People always have secrets of some kind, it seems to me."

*　*　*

Jace wheeled his truck into the drive at Camille's house. He knocked...hard...but no one answered. Maybe she hadn't come back after all. As he was preparing to leave, he heard faint music coming from the back deck. He walked around the house and found her sitting cross-legged on the wooden flooring while she stared at the mountains in the distance.

"Emily or Camille or whoever you are," he began in a rather loud voice.

Startled, she turned to look up at him. She acknowledged his presence and said softly, "Jace." With the next breath, she told him, "The name's Camille."

He stood there for a minute, unsure of what to say next. She looked like a little girl with her hair pulled back and a ball cap on. If there had been any make-up, it was probably washed off by the tears he thought he saw when he first walked up.

"I wanted to give this back to you," he said as he tossed the check on her lap. "As it turned out, it wasn't needed. Some good friends paid for the band and their accommodations. I could have destroyed it but I wanted to give it back in person and tell you I don't appreciate being used. You only pretended to enjoy our dates so you'd have material for your magazine."

In the same monotone voice, she answered him, "And you only dated me because you knew I had money and could bail your ass out of a jam. It would seem as though we used each other, Jace. I guess you could call it double deception, don't you think? By the way, you're welcome and I'm happy the weekends were a success."

She returned her gaze to the mountains and he sat down beside her.

"Look, Camille. I came here today prepared to let you know how angry I've been at you. I know we had a few dates but in my recollection, none of them ended up like you wrote...or even close to it. I am pretty naïve about the publishing world, but can you explain the whole situation to me? I like you and to tell the truth, I laughed when I first read about our imaginary escapades but if Maggie figured out who you were writing about, I'm sure there are others who will, too. And there's one woman in particular that I don't want to see your article, y'know?"

She took a deep breath. "I'll make this as succinct as possible, Jace. My magazine was experiencing declining numbers. Sort of like your bar. I needed something relevant for my readers to pique their interest like you needed Hubie and the band. My staff and I agreed to run a 6-month series of articles on the subject of online dating...specifically of the cougar type...older woman and younger man. Instead of just giving them boring statistics it was decided to send me to some far-off state where no one knew me and I would actually do the online dating. Under an assumed name of course...Emily Hasbro. I liked you and enjoyed our dates but I didn't want to lead you on to the point of being serious so I made up that part. End of story. I'm very sorry if it's become a problem for you. *Mavis' Mag* isn't distributed in this part of the country so it shouldn't show up where your friends can see it. Oh, and this was my mother's house so that's how I ended up in Bozeman."

"It *was* your mother's house? It isn't hers any longer?" he asked.

"No. It's mine now. She died a few weeks ago and left it to me."

'Way to go, Jace. Put your big foot in your mouth. Maybe she came back to grieve and you come to attack her. Good job.'

"I'm so sorry. Sorry about your mother dying and sorry I showed up when I did. Please accept my apologies. I'll go now and don't worry about the article. You did what you had to do...it wasn't illegal or immoral so forget it. I hope you decide to stay in Bozeman."

Collier was on his way to his next job when he saw a vehicle in Camille's drive. As he came closer, he saw a second one...Jace's truck. Just as he began to turn in, Jace came around the side of the house. He walked to Collier's truck and indicated Collier should roll down the window.

"Hello Jace. What are you doing here?"

"I came to return something of Camille's. She's on the back deck and if I were you, I'd go back there and talk to her. I think she could use a shoulder to cry on...maybe."

With that, he got into his truck and left. Collier wasn't sure what to do. He had no idea Camille was back. If she wanted to see him, she certainly could have contacted him and let him know she was coming.

CHAPTER 41

COLLIER SAT IN his truck in the drive for a few minutes, debating what he should do. She left without a word...not a goodbye note, not a text...nothing. Are you going to throw a possible future away because your pride is hurt? Be an adult, Collier.'

He stepped onto the deck and sat down beside her without saying a word. She was looking at the mountains in the distance and occasionally, she would turn a snow globe over and watch the snow fall. Neither of them spoke but eventually, she placed her hand on his knee.

"Have you come to chastise me for my actions, also, Collier?"

"No, Camille. I came to sit with you for a bit...plain and simple. I didn't know you were back until Jace told me when I saw him out front."

She nodded slowly and turned the globe over again.

"My mother left me this property and this snow globe. One portrays her wealth and one symbolizes her frustration with me when I was a child and...my entire life."

They sat in silence for an extended period of time. He put his arm around her shoulders and drew her close. "Have you shed any tears over your mother's death yet?"

"No and I don't expect to. I didn't shed any tears all the years I was a lonely kid and knew without a doubt, she never wanted me, so I don't think one lengthy letter will change that."

Collier didn't know what letter she was talking about but he let it pass.

"The articles you wrote for your magazine…I assume you know or have heard that Maggie is certain one is about Jace and one is about me."

"Have you read them?" she asked.

"No but I was told the one supposedly depicting your evening with Jace is pretty descriptive, for lack of a better word."

"Yes, it is. I used our few kisses as an opener and then built the rest of it…all fictitious."

"Why didn't you embellish the one that's supposed to be about me?"

She turned to him and without blinking, she stated, "I didn't want to imagine what our time together would be like, Collier. I wanted to experience it firsthand. I wanted to live it, not write about it."

"I'd like that too, Camille."

Turning the globe, she told him, "I began living a lie the day I set foot in Montana. I didn't tell you the entire truth about anything. Just as this snow falls and then needs to be turned over again, I need to turn over some things in my life. I want to tell you everything about me but not today, okay?"

"Would you like to revisit the place we went on my friend's ranch? If you remember, it's a perfect spot for talking and thinking."

She nodded. He helped her up and put his arms around her. "Trust me, Camille. I'll never intentionally hurt you. Can we go tomorrow?"

"Yes, I'd like that."

He turned her toward him and kissed her…softly at first but when she put her hands behind his head and pulled him in, the kiss became more intense.

As he backed out of the drive and headed down the street, he glanced in his rear view mirror and saw another vehicle pull into Camille's driveway. A man got out and entered the house but he was too far away to see who it was.

*   *   *

Jace returned to *The Branding Iron* as Will was leaving. "Larry sent me home for the day but I'll be back in the morning."

"Sounds good."

Maggie met him as soon as he entered the door. "Don't sit down, Jace. Get your tail end to Dani's house."

"Why? What happened? Is she okay?"

As she was pushing him out the door and back into his truck, she explained as best as she could what took place while he was gone. "Listen, Boss, you and I both know how you feel about that gal, ever since you went to Colorado with her. You tried the online dating mostly because you were forced to but your heart was never in it. Now take my advice and go tell her how much she means to you."

'Well, you are doing a bang-up job of screwing things up, Maggie.'

*   *   *

Jace drove to Dani's house trying to think of the words he was going to say to convince her he had not been intimate with Camille. Nothing came to mind except the truth so he would give it a shot.

When he knocked on the door, Dean answered but didn't look too happy to see him.

"I need to talk to Dani. Is she here?"

"She's in the barn. Probably talking things over with her horse. She's done that since she was a little girl. But if you want my advice...tread softly. I don't take kindly to anyone hurting her."

"I will, I promise." He walked to the barn and found Dani. She didn't hear him approaching but he heard her talking as she brushed her mare.

"How could I be so stupid to think maybe he cared about me? I can't compete with an older woman who has all kinds of experience. And obviously, that's what Jace wants."

"Dani?" She whirled around and he ducked to miss being hit with the brush she'd been using.

"Whoa...wait a minute. I want to say a few things to you but I'd like to keep my head in place, if you don't mind."

"I don't want to hear anything you have to say, Jace Matthews. Now get off my property. I'm a very good shot with a rifle and I haven't had any target practice for a while, but you might do."

"Okay, Annie Oakley, I'm going," he said as he raised his hands. "But not until you hear what I have to say."

"Talk," was her answer to him.

He did his best to explain what she read in the magazine. "Dani, she made it up to make it more interesting for her readers. It wasn't true. I did kiss her the night I took her home but that was as far as it went. I have been in love with you since we went to Colorado but I didn't think you'd be interested in an old man like me."

She narrowed her eyes and didn't smile. "Old man? You think forty-two is an old man?"

"It seems like it when the woman you want is only thirty."

He took a step closer but she backed up.

"I can't compete with a sophisticated older woman who has class, looks and experience."

"There is no competition. It took me a while to realize it, but you're the only person I've been thinking about for months."

Jace took another step toward her. This time she couldn't back up as she was against the stall wall. He reached for her and pulled her close. She let her arms drop and put her head on his chest. He raised her chin so she was looking up at him. Then he kissed her like he'd wanted to do since they first met.

*   *   *

True to his word, Collier arrived on time for their short journey. Camille climbed in bringing bottles of water and a few snacks. They were both quiet on the way until he asked, "Who was the man I saw come to your house yesterday? I'm sorry to ask, but I have to know."

"That was Will. He drove out with me and he's staying at the house for a while."

Collier looked straight ahead. "This is the Will you were married to?"

"Yes. One and the same." Camille explained their relationship the same way Will had explained it to Maggie. "I know it's hard to believe, Collier but this is the truth with a capital T. We are good friends...nothing more. We had a stormy marriage but once we divorced, we became friends. There's never been any intimacy since the divorce was final."

He took a deep breath and exhaled slowly. "You're asking me to believe something I'm struggling with."

"I can't force you to believe me. That's your choice."

When they reached their destination, they sat as they had the first time...contemplating the beauty spread out in front of them.

"Do you remember what I said about my faith the last time we were here?"

"Yes," Camille said. "I do and I envy you. I'd like to have a faith like that."

"You can. It's not something you buy at the mall...it's in your heart."

"My heart is a mess right now. Did I mention at the memorial service, if you can call it that, I met my father? I'm fifty-six years old and just now met him...surreal, isn't it?"

"I can't even imagine but how did that go?"

A half smile teased her lips. "What can I say? We were both at a loss for words. I mean, think about it...what do you say? 'Hi Dad, nice to meet you. Want to have lunch some time?'"

"The humorous thing is we did have lunch. He described the Barbara he knew when they were young. She was the one who set the boundaries and refused to allow him to see me. She didn't want or need him or his money. When she knew she was dying, she contacted him and asked him to meet me and check on me occasionally. Just so I would know I wasn't an orphan. Still trying to be in control...dead or alive." She shook her head slightly. "She was a manipulator, extraordinaire."

They spent the next few hours discussing their lives, their likes and dislikes and their differences.

At one point, Collier asked what kept her from actually spending the night with some of the men she dated for her articles.

"My first response was going to be that I was a writer, not a slut but I know that's not what you were implying. My answer is in another one of the columns for my readers to see and I believe their responses are indicative of most 'cougars.' We have fears tied to our insecurities about ourselves and our images. It's much easier to make love to a man the same age as you because you're most likely in the same physical condition.

But when the female is older, she thinks of things like: will he notice my breasts aren't exactly perky any longer or how do I hide this roll around my middle or will he notice the scar I have or the stretch marks on my belly and a myriad of other thoughts. You get the idea. The strange thing is most older men don't think about similar things when they're with a younger woman."

Collier started laughing. "I'm sorry but I can't imagine thinking those thoughts about someone I loved. If I wanted to make love to her, I wouldn't care about any of that."

"That's good to know, Collier."

Chapter 42

"TELL ME WHAT you think when you're done eating." Will told Maggie as he set a plate containing a perfect omelet in front of her.

He sat down next to her while she devoured it. "I was thinking that maybe *The Branding Iron* should offer more in the way of selections than just bar food."

She didn't answer but continued eating.

"You know, maybe not breakfast but perhaps a few steak selections or a pasta dish or two."

She wiped her lips with her napkin and asked, "And who is going to prepare these dishes? The omelet was delicious but steaks are a whole different ballgame."

He smiled. "I told you I was a fry cook while I was in college but I neglected to tell you I spent several years as a sous chef at a prestigious restaurant. I decided I could make more money in the stock exchange business so I changed careers."

"You need to discuss this with Jace, not me. Personally, I don't think our kitchen is big enough to accomodate the kind of equipment you might need, but what do I know? I'm a bartender."

"And the best in the country." Jace said as he walked in on their conversation. He glanced at the empty plate in front of Maggie and raised his eyebrows. "Are we serving breakfast now or just to special people?" he asked as he looked at Will.

"Sit down Jace. Will has something he'd like to discuss with you."

"That's good because I have something I'd like to discuss with him."

*   *   *

"Dad, what was the age difference between you and Mom?" Dani asked her father.

"I was six years older than her. Why?"

"Jace seems to think our age difference is a problem."

"How do you feel about it? Is it a problem for you?"

"No. I know twelve years is a big gap but he's still young and healthy."

Dean laughed at that. "Sounds like you're describing a horse, Dani, not a man you're falling in love with."

"I didn't say I was in love with him, Dad."

"Yes, you did...in a lot of subtle ways."

*   *   *

"Dani, I'd like your opinions on a few ideas I've been tossing around in my head."

She nodded as she sipped her iced tea. "Sure, go ahead. I'm always willing to give my opinion, Jace although you may not like it sometimes."

He smiled at her before he leaned over and kissed her quickly. "I know, but whether I like your input or not, I like you...a lot."

She grinned. "So what's your idea or did you forget it already?"

"Dani, truthfully, you make me forget everything except how happy I am when we're together. Now where was I?...Oh yeah, my ideas. I believe Will is an exceptionally talented cook, chef…whatever you want to call him…and he seems to genuinely enjoy the work. We couldn't remodel *The Branding Iron* due to city codes and expense but I think there's an abundance of unused or underused space in the kitchen. Perhaps a little readjusting would make it easier to prepare something other than just bar food."

"And why do you want to change the menu?"

"Ever since the two weekends Hubie's band played, we've been full to capacity in the evenings. Now that Ken is taking his 'talent search' job seriously, people seem to enjoy the entertainment he's found but I've heard them talking about the food, too. I want to make certain our new customers keep returning and bring their friends with them."

"I think it's a good idea, Jace. While you're at it, why not make use of Will's expertise and use his input on the best way to implement the changes you're considering?"

He nodded in agreement. "I'll talk to him today. I've also been considering how I can bring my guide business back to life. If you come up with any brilliant thoughts, let me know. Now, my next question is about us."

She cocked her head to one side and gave him a quizzical look. "What about us?"

"I know going steady is a term from my high school years and will undeniably date me but I don't know exactly what else to call it. The point is I don't want to be with anyone but you and I don't want to think about you spending time with Mitch or anyone else either."

"I think that's called being exclusive, Jace."

"Whatever you call it is okay with me, if you'll think about it. I don't want to pressure you or make it sound like a demand, Dani. You've made me happier than I've been in many years and I don't want to lose you."

She placed her hand on top of his. "The only way you'll lose me is if you tell me to leave."

* * *

Camille listened to her messages. The third one was a bit disconcerting. "Camille, it's Allie. I know it's early but I need you to come home right away. It's extremely important."

She couldn't imagine what happened that was that important.

She returned Allie's call and discovered her magazine was being sued by a man whose wife was certain he was being described in one of her columns. She was threatening to divorce him and he was suing *Mavis' Mag* for defamation of character and numerous other complaints.

"Can't our attorneys handle it?"

"They have been but now they're going to need your deposition or possible court appearance. They will be contacting you but I wanted to give you a 'heads up.'"

She thanked Allie and told her she would wait for the attorney's call. Then she called Collier.

"I will most likely be going back to St Louis in the next couple of days. Maybe we could have dinner tonight?"

* * *

Jace knocked on the door. When Dean answered, he looked surprised. "Dani's not here. She went into town to mail a package. You can come in and wait for her if you want to."

"I knew she wasn't here. I wanted to talk to you alone, Dean."

He removed his hat and sat down. "I realize your daughter and I haven't known each other very long but I have fallen hopelessly in love with her. I also am well aware that there's a twelve-year difference in our ages. I'm not going to rush her to marry me but I would like your permission to ask her."

Dean smiled at him. "Dani's mother and I were six years apart. Age means nothing if people love each other. It's all about what's in here," he stated as he tapped his heart. "I probably shouldn't tell you this. Dani doesn't even know but her mom and I only knew each other for a month before I asked her to marry me." He smiled as he remembered. "Boy, Howdy, did her dad pitch a fit."

Jace nodded, picturing it in his mind. Any father would probably be upset.

"Back to the present," Dean said. "As you know, it's just been me and Danielle since she was very young. We've been a team for all those years but it's time she has a life of her own. I like you and respect you, Jace. I give my permission and thanks for humoring an old man by asking me."

* * *

Collier took her to the airport a few days later and kissed her goodbye. He had a sinking feeling he might never see her again. *'That's ridiculous. Why wouldn't she come back? You know how she feels about you. Yeah…but have you told her exactly how you feel about her?'*

After he saw her plane leave, he went to *The Branding Iron* and ordered a beer.

Maggie looked at him and whispered, "What's up with that 'hang dog' face, Collier? Did you lose your best friend?" she teased.

"Yes. Maybe I did. I hadn't thought about it in those terms but…thanks, Maggie."

She watched him leave and wondered what she said that solicited that response.

*   *   *

Camille spent several days with attorneys discussing the ridiculous charges. She didn't feel there should be a case let alone any admission of guilt. Suddenly before the papers were signed, the attorneys called to tell her all charges had been dropped. It was over.

She'd been doing a lot of thinking while she was 'home' in St. Louis. As she sat in her townhouse, she realized it didn't feel like home any longer. By the same thought process, Bozeman, Montana didn't feel like a temporary vacation spot...despite the deceptions and deceit, it had become 'home' to her. Perhaps she should consider keeping the property in Bozeman, instead of placing it on the market. It was entirely too big for one person. She would pray about some clarity on the subject.

'Pray about it? Collier, and perhaps your father, must be rubbing off on you, Camille. You've never considered praying about any decision in the past. Maybe that's why many of them weren't good decisions.'

She laughed at her own thoughts. As she got ready for bed, she realized she wasn't looking forward to going back to the office tomorrow. Somehow, the magazine had lost its appeal. Maybe when she got there, she'd feel as she always had.

*   *   *

Camille entered the staff meeting to applause and greetings of congratulations.

"I want you to know I've missed being here and seeing all of you but first things first," she told them. "The man decided to withdraw his lawsuit in light of some details I provided. He may still be getting a divorce but it has to do with the fact he was even on a dating site. His wife wasn't impressed." Everyone laughed and applauded.

"We want you to know how much we missed our 'cougar' and we're very impressed with the articles you sent," Jack stated. "It must be tough having a different date every night."

Camille smiled and said, "It is a hard job but as they say…somebody's gotta do it."

The secretary interrupted the meeting by sticking her head in the door while trying to apologize. "I'm terribly sorry, Ms. Desmond but there's some man out here wearing a cowboy hat and he says he has to see you."

Before she could answer, Collier pushed past the secretary, picked Camille up and twirled her around. Then he set her down and got on one knee in front of her.

Looking up at her, he said, "This cowboy wants to know if the cougar will marry him."

He opened a box with a ring in it and held it out to her.

The room was deafeningly quiet while she bent down and kissed him. Then she pulled him to his feet and looking into his face, she told him, "Yes, this cougar will marry the cowboy."

Made in the USA
Lexington, KY
12 July 2018